Single
GIRL RULES
#THREE HEADED MONSTER

IVY SMOAK

Single Girl Rule #3

Never let a friend go into a bathroom alone.

Chapter 1

HERE HE COMES!

Saturday, Sept 14, 2013

I awoke to the sound of weird mouth noises.

Is Ash blowing one of my bodyguards?

She had really come out of her shell last night so it wouldn't surprise me that much. But no, she was just moving her mouth around and rubbing her jaw.

"What are you doing?" I asked as I shielded my eyes from the morning sun streaming into our dorm.

She wiggled her jaw again and shot an angry look at the loaf of banana bread on her nightstand. "Can you get tetanus from banana bread? My jaw hurts like hell. And my face feels…stiff."

"No, it's not tetanus. It's just a sign that you threw me the best bachelorette party ever."

She looked confused. "How is this the sign of a good bachelorette party? Did we have an epic food fight that I'm somehow forgetting? Because it feels like I smeared a banana all over my face."

"That's a nice PG-13 way to sum up what happened," I said with a laugh. And then I rubbed my jaw too. "Ow. I forgot how much this hurts. It's been forever since I got cockjaw."

"Lockjaw?" gasped Ash. "I thought you said it wasn't tetanus!"

"No, silly. *Cock*jaw. As in…when your jaw hurts from sucking too many cocks."

Ash stared at me for a good five seconds. And then she laughed. "Oh my God," she said between laughs. "For a second I thought you were being serious."

"Girl, don't pretend like you don't remember sucking off those strippers last night. You were amazing!"

Ash laughed again.

Is she still drunk?

"I'm gonna go shower," she said. "My face is gonna be a mess if I don't scrub this banana off ASAP. You know how sensitive my skin is."

A good face-full of cum always had me glowing the next day. But Ash did have unusually sensitive skin. Whenever we did something new, or talked to strangers, or were anywhere near hot guys her face always turned bright red. I had no idea what caused it.

She grabbed her towel and stepped around a plate of banana bread. "And if you clean up, save a little banana bread. I need to send a sample to a lab to test for tetanus. I had a feeling one of those bananas had turned…"

I nodded. But I'd stopped listening after the bit about "If you clean up." What kind of basic bitch would clean up after their own bachelorette party? Or…ever? I had men for that. I was honestly a little surprised that getting males to clean for you wasn't a Single Girl Rule.

Speaking of which…

I pulled out my list of the Single Girl Rules and scanned down them.

Rule #1: Boys are replaceable, friends are forever.

Check. Ash and I were besties. No boys would ever get between us.

Rule #2: Girls' night is every Friday. No exceptions.

It would take a lifetime to truly check this one off. But my bachelorette party last night had been the most epic first girls' night ever. So until next Friday rolled around, Rule #2 was complete.

Rule #3: Never let a friend go into a bathroom alone.

Hmm… Most of the Single Girl Rules made perfect sense. But this one… This one was a real head-scratcher.

"Teddybear!" I yelled.

He cracked the door and poked his head in. "Yes?"

"I need your help."

"Of course." He licked his lips to moisten them and then got on his knees by my bed.

"I like the way you think. But that will have to wait. My mind is too preoccupied by a most unsolvable quandary."

"Oh." He stood up, looking rather disappointed. "If you need help with calculus, you'll have to wait for Ghost to return with breakfast."

I laughed. Why in the world would I still be learning calculus? I was a freshman in college, not a sixth-grader. "It's Single Girl Rule #3: Never let a friend go into a bathroom alone. What could that possibly mean?"

"That's just classic girl code."

I stared at him.

"You know… To protect each other from being raped. Or kidnapped. You of all people should understand that quite well after last night."

I shook my head. "You're starting to sound like Ghost with all this kidnapping talk. But the Single Girl Rules wouldn't include such a dark and gloomy rule. They're about living your best life. Not living in fear."

"Then maybe it's in there because the bathroom is a perfect place to gossip about guys. Or to help each other fix your makeup?"

"Well now you're just being ridiculous. Because there's nothing to gossip about until you've run off to bang a hot stud in the bathroom. Same goes for makeup. Why fix it if a delicious cumshot hasn't ruined it yet?"

"In that case, maybe it's just a really roundabout way for the rules to suggest that you spice it up and bang guys in more unique locations. And then you can run to the bathroom after to talk about it."

"Oooh. So it's saying to have more sex in public? I freaking love that." My mind started spinning with all the best public sex places on campus. "Oooh. Tonight you should bend me over that adorable little fountain on the green."

His eyes lit up. But then his face fell. "I'm not sure Chad would appreciate that."

"What does he have against fountains? I guess we could do it in a lecture hall instead. Oh! Like we were teaching a sex position class. Now that would be a class worth attending. Unlike English."

"It wasn't the fountain that I thought Chad would take issue with."

"Then what's the problem?"

"He's your boyfriend."

"And…?" I asked.

"And he'd be pissed if you cheated on him."

"Who said anything about cheating? It's not like I'm going to fire you and take you out to a romantic dinner first."

"Is that what it would take to make it cheating?"

"Yes. Well, maybe. It would still be a kind of a gray area since Chad would get to watch. And I have some hall passes that I could use. AND I'd obviously ask Chad to fuck me against the fountain first. But I already know he'd pass."

Teddybear looked shocked. "How could he possibly say no to that? Sounds like someone has a bad case of stage fright."

"Hmmm…kinda. What's the opposite of that?"

"Premature ejaculation in public?"

"There's gotta be a more elegant name for it. But yeah, that's about right. It happened once and now he's super scared to try it again." I pulled out my phone and texted Chad: "Hey babe! Wanna bend me over the fountain on the green tonight?"

He texted back a second later. "God, I love when you tell me exactly what you want. But I'll have to take a raincheck. I already have plans for us tonight."

"See?" I said, showing the text to Teddybear. "He's too scared."

I quickly texted Chad back: "Well whenever you get back here, come right in. The door is unlocked. I need to hear all about your sexy plans for us tonight." And once I found out, I'd make them better. Sometimes Chad made the worst plans. Nothing I couldn't fix though.

I looked back up at Teddybear. "It's ironic how Chad just complimented my directness immediately before acting like a little bitch and not fessing up to being scared." Then something clicked. "Wait a second! We've got Rule #3 all wrong!"

"Huh?"

"The rules are as direct as I am. And they certainly aren't shy about sex. If Rule #3 was about public sex, it would say it. Thus we have it all wrong."

"Damn, you're right. But I still think we should try that fountain thing."

I pushed his arm. "Teddybear! You're so bad. I have a boyfriend!"

"But…"

"Maybe you could do it with Ash instead. She's single and definitely ready to mingle. You should have seen her sucking off those strippers last night. Girl has skills."

"I don't think Ash…"

"Shhh." I put my finger to his lips. "I think I figured out Rule #3!"

"You did?"

"Yes. Look at rules 1 and 2. They're all about friends. Rule #1 comes right out and says that friends are forever. And Rule #2 is all about making time for your friends."

"Right. Which is why I guessed that it's about protecting your friends from rape. Or gossiping with them. Or doing makeup together."

I laughed. "No, no, no. Rule #3 is about helping your friends get laid. If you see a friend going to the bathroom alone, send a hot stud in after them to fuck their brains out. It makes perfect sense!"

"Are you sure?"

"I've never been so sure of anything in my entire life. I can't wait to go tell Ash." I grabbed my towel and started for the door. "Wait a second! Ash is in the bathroom right now. Alone. Which means I need to send her a hot stud." I stared at Teddybear, but he didn't move.

"Why are you staring at me like that?"

"Did you not hear what I just said?"

"That you need to send Ash a stud."

"Right. So why are you still sitting in this room when you should be railing my bestie against the shower wall?" God, Ash was going to love this. The things Teddybear could do with his tongue…he had to be shared.

His eyes got big. "You want me to fuck Ash? Because a week ago you blackmailed me and Ghost to make us back off because our presence was scaring her."

"I thought you were scaring her. But I had it all wrong. You two watching her change was making her so horny. The poor girl must have been going to class every day with her panties completely soaked."

Teddybear stood up a little straighter. "Really?"

"Yup. Now let's hurry before she's done her shower." I pulled him down the hall to the women's restroom. The shower was still going. *Perfect!*

"Ready?" I whispered to Teddybear.

"You really think this is a good idea?" he asked.

"When have I ever been wrong about anything?"

"Never?"

"Exactly. Now take your clothes off." I stood back and admired his chiseled body as he stripped off his tight T-shirt and slacks. It was so tempting to just bring him into the shower with me for our usual morning routine. But today I had to share.

I grabbed his cock the second it was out of his boxer briefs. My other hand ran up his sixpack and wrapped behind the back of his neck. And then I pulled his head down until his ear was right by my lips.

"You ready to fuck my bestie?" I whispered, letting my lips brush against his ear. He stiffened in my hand. "I bet you've dreamt about sinking your hands into her red hair as she bobs up and down on your cock." I lightly bit his earlobe and he groaned. "Or are you just gonna grab her tiny little waist and fuck her against the cold tiles?" I would have kept going, but I didn't want him to burst in my hand.

I let go of him and knocked on the shower door.

"Present," yelled Ash at the top of her lungs.

Present? "Ash, it's me. I have a surprise for you."

"A surprise? What kind of surprise?"

"It's a surprise. Open up."

"Just toss it over the door."

Odd request. "Are you sure?"

"Yes."

"Okay… It's coming over in three…" I knelt down and put my hands together to form a step for Teddybear.

"I really don't know if this is a good idea," he whispered. "She seems a little jumpy."

"Trust me. It'll be fine."

He hesitantly stepped onto my hand and I leaned forward to make sure his throbbing cock hit me in the face. Ash was a lucky girl this morning.

"Two…"

Teddybear grabbed the top of the shower door and got ready to hoist himself up.

"One! Here he comes!"

I pushed my hands up to give Teddybear a little extra oomph. But I may have underestimated the force that he was already exerting to get himself up, because my extra oomph sent him *hurtling* over the door into the shower.

Chapter 2
THE SHOWER PERVERT
Saturday, Sept 14, 2013

"AHHHHHHHHHH!" screamed Ash. I'd never heard something so ear piercing. The shower door flew open and Ash ran out, full nude and still screaming at the top of her lungs. A second later she was out of the bathroom, but I could still hear her screaming down the hall.

"Ow," muttered Teddybear as he tenderly held his junk.

I looked back and forth between him and the bathroom door. "I think your over-the-shower-door entry might have been a tad aggressive. Thoughts?"

He groaned.

"Are you okay?" I asked.

"Her knees are so bony."

"Well what were you doing with her knees? No wonder she was so freaked out! Next time start with her tits, you pervert."

"She kneed me."

"And deservedly so. Seriously, dude. You can't just go grabbing at a girls' knees all willy-nilly. That's a very delicate area. Do you know how long it takes to heal an ACL?"

"I didn't go for her knees!"

"I know." I stifled a laugh. "I'm just messing with you. This one is totes on me. And to make up for it, I'll let you bend me over the fountain sometime."

His eyes lit up.

"But maybe not tonight, because it sounds like Chad has something planned. And I might have to take Ash to therapy. I don't want her to freak out when we try this again tomorrow morning."

"What?!"

"Oh, and don't worry, I'll let Ash know this was a Single Girl Rule thing, so she'll understand. Maybe wait a bit before you come back to the room though so she has time to calm down. But don't take too long, because there's a shit ton of banana stuff you need to clean up." I spun on my heel and walked out of the bathroom.

I couldn't wait to explain what happened to Ash. She was gonna think it was hilarious. But in the meantime…I had a feeling that it would be smart to enter the room *very* slowly. Actually, entering at all would probably be a bad idea. A gentle knock accompanied by a note passed under the door would probably be the safest approach. Because even though Ash appeared sweet and innocent, I knew that deep down she was a feisty bitch.

Which meant that things were about to go *very* badly for whoever was at our door.

Chad?

"Chad!" I called. But it was a second too late.

He opened the door and walked in.

Ash screamed, "DIE, PERVERT!!!!!!"

Chad covered his face and screamed louder. And much much higher pitched. And then he ran out of the room and face first into the wall across the hall.

I ran over and got there just in time to prevent Ash from jumping on him.

"Chastity!" she yelled. "Be careful! He's a filthy shower pervert." She held up pepper spray in one hand and a loaf of banana bread in the other in a very threatening manner.

"Whoa," I said. "Put the banana bread down. And the pepper spray. It's just Chad."

"Your boyfriend?"

I nodded my head. "You've met him before. And he's not the shower pervert."

Chad was hunched over in a ball crying. But I was pretty sure he was fine. I'd pepper sprayed tons of guys. It didn't kill them or anything.

Ash looked back and forth between us. "Hmm...you're right. The shower pervert was naked." Then she squinted at me. "And wait a second. You were there too. And you said something about having a surprise for me."

"So...funny story. The shower pervert was Teddybear. And I was the one who put him up to it. But I promise it came from a good place."

"Chastity! Why on Earth would you do that?"

"Rule #3: Never let a friend go into a bathroom alone. Teddybear and I were talking and we figured out that it means you should always send a hot stud into the bathroom if your friend goes in alone."

"Wow. That is definitely not what Rule #3 means. It's so no one gets kidnapped. Or...worse."

"It's open to debate."

Ash shook her head and looked over at Chad. He was still curled up on the ground holding his eyes. "Chad, I'm so sorry. I didn't mean to attack you. I thought you were a deranged pervert."

"Well you're right about him being a pervert," I said. "He should really learn not to barge into women's rooms unannounced."

"You told me that the door was unlocked and to come right in," Chad groaned.

Did I? Hmm...that did sound a little familiar. *Oopsies.*

"I need water," he croaked.

"Let's see the damage." I moved his hands away from his eyes. His whole face was red and puffy and covered in tears. "Wow, Ash. You must have hit him right in the sweet spot. Great technique." I put my hand up for a high-five.

Ash reluctantly high-fived me. "Shouldn't we be helping him?"

I waved her off. "He'll be fine. He just needs boobs. #BoobsFixEverything. Here...help me drag him into our room."

We each hooked an arm under his and dragged him in. A quick wipe with one of my makeup erasers got most of the pepper spray away from his eyes, and then I pulled my shirt off and let him bury his face in my tits.

"All better?" I asked after he'd been down there for like fifteen minutes.

He shook his head. "Not yet. But I think a back massage might help."

"Well now you're just milking it. So what is it that you have planned for tonight?"

He looked up at me from between my beautiful breasts. *God, I'm so hot.* Chad was so lucky to have me.

"Babe?" he asked.

"What?"

"Do you wanna come?"

"Come where? Sorry, I got distracted by my tits." I drummed on the tops of them. "Do you think they're getting bigger?"

He smiled up at me. "Definitely. But as I was saying...my roommate helped me get punched by the Gryphon Club. And they're throwing a party tonight to mingle with potential pledges."

"And you want me to come help you impress them?"

"Exactly." He checked his watch. "Shit. It's getting late, but if we leave now, we should make it just in time."

I stared at him. "Is the party in London?"

"No?"

"Then why do we need to leave now? It's only like an hour flight to Boston."

"Right. But I drove. And I can't just leave my car here."

"Why not?" I asked.

"It's a Porsche."

"And…what's the issue? Just buy a new one."

Chad shook his head like I was being ridiculous. "I'm not gonna do that."

"Well you can't seriously think that I'd ride in a car for *six* hours. No one does that."

"Babe, come on. It'll be a fun little road trip."

"Ew. What are we, homeless?"

"Road trips aren't only for homeless people."

"Hmm… No, I'm pretty sure they are. Right, Ash?"

"Yup," she said absentmindedly. For some reason she was sitting at her desk ignoring us.

"See?" I said, pushing his face out of my cleavage. He didn't deserve my boobs after suggesting something so awful.

"Well if you don't want to drive, do you have a better solution?"

"Of course I do. We can take Daddy's fun jet."

"But my car…"

"Teddybear will drive it back for you."

He nodded. "That's actually a good plan."

"I know." I smiled at him and started packing all the outfits I might need. By the end of this weekend, everyone in the Gryphon Club was gonna know that Chad has the hottest girlfriend in the world.

Chapter 3

#WORSTPOSITIONEVER

Saturday, Sept 14, 2013

"Who wore it better?" I asked as I emerged from the airplane bathroom in my sexy little flight attendant uniform. "Me or Esme?"

Ash and Slavanka looked up.

"Whoa," said Ash. "You look hot."

"Too much button," said Slavanka.

I looked down. *Hmm...* I'd originally buttoned it up enough to hide my bra. But Slavanka had a point. When it came to cleavage, more was more.

I popped the top button off. "Better?"

Slavanka nodded. "Yes, yes."

"So does that mean that it looks better on me than Esme?"

"I can't really judge until I see Esme too," said Ash.

"She and Zoraida have the day off. Which is weird, because I didn't think Daddy ever gave flight attendants time off. But it worked out kind of perfectly, because I've always thought I'd look amazing in this uniform."

Ash's eyes got big. "Wait. So you're our only flight attendant today?"

"Yup!"

"Oh God," said Ash. "What if we crash? Do you even know how to deploy the emergency slide? Or what position babies need to be in to brace for impact?"

I put my hand on my hip. "Trick question. Everyone knows that babies are the first thing you throw overboard if the plane starts losing altitude. The decreased weight helps the plane stabilize, and the lack of crying babies allows everyone to focus on saving themselves."

Ash stared at me in horror. "I just remembered I had a…thing today with…that person. I better get off this plane immediately."

"No way," I said. "Not until we know for sure what Rule #3 means. I mean, this is Rule #3 we're talking about. It made the top five. It must be really important. And just imagine how many bathrooms you'd potentially go into alone this weekend if we were in different cities. As your bestie, I can't allow it."

"I'd rather risk that than fly in this death trap with a baby-tossing stewardess from hell."

"Gah, fine. I won't toss any babies. If it makes you feel better, I actually know everything about the safety procedures for this plane. We'll be fine. Plus there are no babies on board."

"Oh really?" Ash grabbed a safety pamphlet and opened it up. "Then how many life vests are on board?"

"Fifteen. Plus three in the cockpit."

"And where is the closest exit in case of a crash landing?"

I pointed to the main door. "Unless it's a water landing." I walked over to the emergency doors over the wing. "In which case, we must exit onto the wing."

"Wow, you really do know your stuff."

"Of course I do. #PrivatePlaneLife." I was about to ask her for more brain busters, but Chad's green Porsche was approaching on the tarmac. I rushed out and waved to him from the top of the stairs.

I could see him mouth the words *hot damn* when he saw me. Which was exactly the reaction I'd been hoping for.

"Welcome aboard Daddy's fun jet, sir," I said as Chad took the stairs two at a time.

"You look so fucking hot," he said and leaned in for a kiss.

I pushed him away. "Excuse me, sir! Kissing flight attendants is strictly forbidden on this flight." I made a show of straightening my uniform, which drew Chad's eyes directly to my amazing cleavage. "And my eyes are up here. Now please go find your seat and prepare for takeoff."

I smacked his cute little tush as he walked past me. Then I waved goodbye to Teddybear - now in the driver's seat of Chad's Porsche - and secured the airplane door.

***

"Drinks?" I asked as I passed out the menus.

"Oooh," said Ash. "I need more of that banana juice in my life."

Wow. I was all for pre-gaming, but it was only like one in the afternoon. Ash was really coming out of her shell!

"I drink vodka," said Slavanka.

I took the menus and disappeared into the kitchenette. I figured Slavanka could handle her vodka just fine so I gave her a nice healthy glass. But Ash on the other hand... She probably needed a day to cool down after last night. So I just put a little splash of banana juice into a glass of water.

I brought their drinks out to them and then turned my attention to Chad. "And for you, sir?"

"I'll have a blowjob," he said, pointing to *blowjob* on the menu.

Of course you will. "Excellent choice. Please come with me." I grabbed his hand and led him towards the bedroom at the back of the plane.

"Have fun with friendboy," called Slavanka to me.

Friendboy? Wait a second! Slavanka had translated the Single Girl Rules. And she didn't have the best command of English. What if there had been a translation error? For example…what if she'd translated boyfriend as friend. That would mean that Rule #3 was really: Never let a *boy*friend go into a bathroom alone. Which made total sense. The rules were calling for more bathroom sex! *I knew it!*

Rather than continuing to the bedroom, I grabbed Chad's lapel and pushed him into the bathroom.

He stumbled backwards until his butt was pressed against the sink. Which wasn't much of a stumble, because the bathroom was quite small. Daddy really needed to upgrade to a bigger fun jet.

I locked the door and then turned to Chad. He was already unbuttoning his baby-blue shorts. Or trying to. His hands were shaking too much from his excitement. He was clearly in need of assistance. And as his flight attendant this afternoon…that was my job.

I dropped to my knees and shoved his hands out of the way. A second later his shorts fell to his ankles. He moaned as I wrapped my bright red lips around his cock.

It was even smaller than I remembered.

Back in high school I'd thought he was an okay size. But after getting fucked by a real man last night, and having Teddybear and Ghostie at my beck and call at all hours, I now knew that Chad was definitely on the smaller end of the spectrum. #SadPenisFacts. It didn't even go into my throat when I went all the way down.

But it still must have felt amazing for him, because he groaned, "Oh God," and gripped the sink like it was the only thing keeping him from completely losing control.

I slowed down a little to help him from skeeting too soon. And then I heard the rip of foil. A condom rapper fluttered down to the floor.

I looked up at him. "Excuse me, sir. What do you think you're doing with that condom?"

"Getting ready to join the mile-high club."

I opened my mouth in shock. "You ordered a blowjob. That's the second time you've acted completely inappropriate. I have half a mind to land this plane right now and kick your ass off. But luckily you're really handsome. And my boyfriend lives out of town, so I've been so fucking horny." I stood up and unbuttoned my jacket. Then I slid out of my skirt, leaving only my white lingerie.

Chad put the condom on and then hooked his fingers into my panties. But when he pulled them down, they got stuck on my garters.

"What the hell?" he muttered, trying again to pull them down.

"Just rip them off. I want you to fucking dominate me." I bit my lip.

He pulled on either side of them, but he wasn't strong enough.

Dude! Come on!

He tried again. But his face was getting red from straining.

"I got it." I pushed him away and unhooked my garters from my stockings, allowing my panties to slide right down. I tried to kick them away, but there wasn't enough room in this damned bathroom to do it properly.

I pushed Chad out of the way and jumped up onto the sink, with my legs spread invitingly.

Or at least…I thought it was inviting. But Chad just stood there.

"Ready?" I asked.

He nodded.

Then what are you waiting for? I sighed as I grabbed his cock and guided it into me. But he still didn't take charge. He just sat there with it inside of me.

"Is everything okay, sir?" I asked.

"Give me a sec."

I stared at him.

And then he finally started thrusting. But it was way too slow. Or maybe his cock was too small for me to feel it properly. God, I missed the Banana King's thick monster. I moaned just thinking about what he had done to me.

"You like that?" groaned Chad.

"I'd like it even more if you went faster."

"As you wish." He started going *so* fast. Like…too fast. And he was only going back like half an inch on each thrust. It was like being fucked by the world's tiniest jackhammer.

I pushed back against the mirror to try to get him to go deeper. But I couldn't get any purchase on the slick surface. Or maybe he just couldn't go any deeper…

"Harder," I said.

He went back to his slow, boring thrusts.

God damn it! I needed to switch to a position where I was in change. But our options were limited in this little bathroom.

I pushed him backwards onto the toilet. And then I spun around and started riding him reverse cowgirl.

His fingers dug into my hips as I bounced up and down on his cock. But I couldn't really feel much. It kinda seemed like I was just sitting on his lap repeatedly.

"Hold on," he said. "I think it fell out."

What the hell? How was that possible? Dicks didn't just fall out. That wasn't a thing. *Gah, Chad!*

I guided him back in and started again. It went okay for a second, but then Chad tried thrusting at completely the wrong time. So his dick fell out again.

"Just sit back and relax, sir. I'll do all the work."

I reached down to guide him in, but he was all soft and the condom was full of cum.

Well that's disappointing. "Done so soon?" I asked.

"Yeah. I actually finished when you were on the sink. But I kept going to make sure I pleased you too." He gave me a wink.

Say what now? "Handsome *and* thoughtful? That's a rare combination." He was handsome. And maybe thoughtful. But he was fucking terrible at sex.

"Sorry that the second position kinda sucked. I've always thought it looked fun, but the mechanics just don't work."

I shrugged. "You did your best. #WorstPositionEver." *Was it?* I was pretty sure it was amazing. I'd need to try it out with a much bigger cock than Chad's though. Where was Ghost when I needed him? *Oh right, in the cargo hold for safekeeping.* "Welcome to the mile-high club, sir." I straightened his lapel and gave him a kiss on the cheek. Then I pulled on my outfit and left the bathroom.

"I'm no expert," said Ash. "But that seemed fast."

Slavanka shook her head. "So sad. Why you with him?"

"Eh. I've dumped him like ten times. But he doesn't take no for an answer."

Ash nearly spit out her very-watered-down banana juice. "Ten times?"

"Yeah. He's very persistent. Which is actually one of his best qualities."

"And that's why you like him?" asked Ash. "I'm not buying that for one second. I'm pretty sure he secretly has a huge penis. Isn't there a Single Girl Rule about being required by law to tell us if he does? Like uh…Single Girl Rule #35: Dick pics are literally everything. Or something like that?"

"Well, I agree with that statement. #Truth. But that's not a rule."

"Are you sure?" asked Ash.

"You were probably thinking of Rule #9: If you hear about a well-hung man, share the news."

"Ah yeah, that's the one. What's #35 then?"

"If it's been three dates and he hasn't bought you something nice, move on. But now that you mention it, that rule kind of applies here. Because after the third time I dumped Chad, he bought me a pet giraffe to win me back."

"Wow."

"Yeah. He's one of the good ones." I smiled towards the bathroom. "It doesn't matter that his penis is so sad and small."

"Really?" asked Ash. "Because based on literally everything I know about you, I would have thought that would be your #1 criteria."

"No way. Chad is the perfect boyfriend. Other than Daddy, he's the only man I've ever met who loves me for me. It's hard to find a guy like that. It's easy to find randos with big cocks to satisfy me sexually."

"Speaking of being satisfied…what's he still doing in the bathroom?"

"I'm not really sure. Something about needing to wash his junk five times after sex to make sure my lady fluids don't irritate his delicate ball skin. Oh! Also, another thing I love about him is that he's going places. Or at least…he'll be going places if I can impress the guys in the Gryphon Club enough to take a chance on him."

Chapter 4

A PURE DISPLAY OF MASCULINE POWER AND AGILITY
Saturday, Sept 14, 2013

"You guys ready to experience the greatest academic institution ever created?" asked Chad as Daddy's fun jet taxied to a stop.

"Oh no," I said. "Did the pilot accidentally take us back to the University of New Castle?"

Chad looked like his head was going to explode.

"Babe, I'm just joking. I'm so excited to see your dorm and meet your friends and get you into the Gryphon Club."

"It's not that simple. Yes, I got punched. But it's still a long road to initiation."

"Punched?" asked Ash. "I thought they'd outlawed hazing?"

"Not actually punched," I said. "Punched is what it's called at Harvard when you get invited to pledge a final club."

Ash looked at me like I was crazy. "Why don't they just call it pledging a frat?"

Chad gasped. "The Gryphon Club is *not* a frat. I mean...technically it is a fraternity of brothers forever bonded by love and respect."

"Brotherhood of man sex?" asked Slavanka.

I stifled a laugh.

"No!" screamed Chad. "It's...you know what, never mind. Let's just get going." He checked his Rolex. "My boys should be here any minute to give us a ride. Since we flew, we have extra time. And we've planned an amazing afternoon for you girls."

"Ooooh!" I said. "Fun! I can't wait to see the new Odegaard boutique in downtown Boston."

"Huh?" asked Chad. "Who said anything about shopping?"

"I'm pretty sure you did."

"No. This is gonna be even better."

Better than shopping? Boston wasn't known for their spas, but maybe he'd found a hidden gem. And by a hidden gem, I mean a masseur with magical hands and a huge dick.

I rubbed my hands together. "Sounds good to me. Let's go!"

Two guys in plaid shorts and polos with the collars popped were waiting for us on the tarmac. I wasn't sure how long they'd been there, but they'd had enough time to roll out a putting green and light some cigars. The skinny one let out a huge puff of smoke as his overly-jacked friend lined up a putt. The putter looked comically small in his massive hands.

"Hey boys!" I called from the top of the stairs.

The big one totally flubbed his shot. "God damn it!" he yelled, slamming his putter against the green hard enough to bend the shaft. "You can't yell at a man while he's taking a stroke!" He chucked the putter and it went directly through the windshield of an electric blue Lamborghini.

Ash hid behind me.

"Dude," said Chad. "Don't talk to my girl that way."

"I won't if you tell her not to..." The angry guy looked up and his eyes landed on me. The cigar fell out of his mouth. "Sweet lord, Chad. You didn't tell us you were dating a super model."

"Nah," said the skinny guy. "There's no way his girlfriend is that hot. That's just some model he hired to be his flight attendant."

I laughed. "That's very nice of you. But I really am Chad's girlfriend. I'm just dressed up as a flight attendant because Daddy gave the real flight attendants the day off. You must be Chad's friends?"

"Trent Donahue," said the skinny one. "Son of Senator Kenneth Donahue. Democrat, Massachusetts. Vice-chair of the finance committee." He shook my hand with perfect technique.

Well that's a lot of unnecessary information, but okay.

"And this idiot is Scooter."

"Hey girl," grunted the beefy one. "I have something for you." He reached into his back pocket and pulled out a ticket.

I took it and looked down. It had "ADMIT ONE: The Gun Show" printed in jokerman font. "The gun show?" I asked.

When I looked up from the ticket, Scooter flexed. "Welcome to the gun show, baby." He kissed one of his biceps.

Trent let out a sigh. "Why do you always have to be such a douche?"

"Yeah," agreed Chad. "You know girls don't actually find those big muscles attractive, right?"

"Bruh," said Scooter, pinching at Chad's normal sized arms. "Do you even lift?"

Chad swatted him away.

The gentle swat must have hurt, because Scooter started to turn red again and his eyes got all crazy. He picked up Chad and lifted him over his head. I was pretty sure he was about to body slam him onto the hood of the Lambo. But I was much more interested in what I was seeing on his stomach. Because Scooter's shirt had just come untucked, revealing the words SEX MACHINE tattooed just under his naval. The big block letters were wrapped with barbed wire and bookended by two roses in full bloom.

"Please don't kill my boyfriend," I said.

Scooter looked at me and his face got a little less red.

"It would be such a shame if we had to spend all day making funeral arrangements. Then you wouldn't have time to tell Ash all about your workout routine."

Ash nudged me in the ribs. "What are you doing?!" she hissed. "I don't want to know anything about his workouts. He looks like an angry erection!"

She wasn't wrong. But the comparison felt unfair to erections, which were beautiful things. Scooter, on the other hand, was definitely not beautiful. His prematurely balding head looked so tiny on his massive body. Normally I'd be a little enticed by the SEX MACHINE tattoo...but not with Scooter. It just seemed like he was overcompensating.

"Sorry," I whispered back. "It was the only thing I could think of to save Chad from getting Hulk-smashed."

"What we whisper about?" asked Slavanka. "Ash like big beef man?"

"No," said Ash. "No I most certainly do not."

"He very strong," said Slavanka. "He lift Chad so easy." I'd never heard her sound so excited.

Does Slavanka think Scooter is hot? I was all for big muscles. But Scooter was just too much. And more importantly, there was about a 100% chance that he had the world's tiniest little baby penis.

Or maybe the world's second tiniest penis. The way Trent had introduced himself made me think he might take home the gold in that particular contest.

"Alright," said Chad once Scooter had put him down and he'd had ample time to fix his hair in the reflection of one of the non-broken windows of the Lambo. "Everyone ready to get going?"

"Yup," I said. "I just have to change first. How fancy should I go? Are we talking like…a blouse and slacks? Or is it more of a day dress kinda place?"

"It doesn't matter what you wear," said Trent. "Just make sure you packed an extra pair of panties, because yours are gonna be soaked by this display of pure masculine power and agility."

I pressed my thighs together. "Wow. I've never heard a spa described that way, but you've certainly piqued my interest." I pictured myself at the center of a Cirque du Soleil type performance, with various nude masseurs trapezing down to rub me in all the right places.

"We're not going to a spa," said Trent. "We're going to the badminton court. The Wigglesworth Woodshots challenged us to a match. We would have had to forfeit, but now that Chad's back, the match is on. And it's going to be *epic*."

"What happened to us seeing a display of pure masculine power and agility?" I asked.

Trent looked confused. "What do you mean? I just told you. You get to watch us play badminton."

"Hmmm…that's gonna be a hard pass for me." But he'd gotten me all excited to watch hot dudes doing something manly. "Let's go to the football game instead. They're playing Cornell today, right?"

"Yeah, but…" started Trent.

"Babe, please don't make us forfeit to the Wigglesworth Woodshots," said Chad. "We'll be legends if we beat them."

Really? Will you? Because I was pretty sure no badminton match had ever made someone a legend. The only thing legendary about it would be seeing Scooter hold a tiny little racket in his big beefy hands. But staring at hot football players still sounded a million times better. "I guess I can watch your match. It's just a shame that I won't get to wear the sexy cheerleader outfit that I brought. And you know how horny I get eating hotdogs…"

"Okay, we're going to the football game," said Chad.

"Thanks, babe!" I gave him a kiss on the cheek. "Can you grab my suitcases out of the cargo hold?"

"Sure thing." He walked over to the plane and opened the hold. Ghost tumbled out and nearly knocked him over. And for the second time today, Chad screamed bloody murder.

I didn't know when he'd started doing this high-pitched scream, but I was not loving it.

"It's okay," I said. "It's just Ghostie."

"What the hell was he doing in the cargo hold?"

I shrugged. "I think he likes it down there or something. You know how Ghostie gets. Always being so extra."

Ghost growled.

Chad took a moment to compose himself and then crawled into the hold.

"Which suitcase is it?" he called back to me.

"The pink one."

"There are eight of those."

"Just grab them all." I didn't actually bring a cheerleader outfit, but I would make something work. I'd heard some of the football players were in the Gryphon Club, so a sexy little outfit was the perfect way to make a good first impression.

Chapter 5

THE THREE HEADED MONSTER
Saturday, Sept 14, 2013

"Where are we going?" I asked.

"I think I see some seats up there," replied Chad, pointing wayyyyy up to the very back of the stadium.

Say what? I wasn't gonna sit in the back row like a loser. I was gonna sit in the front row. And if I was lucky, the quarterback would notice me and invite me into the locker room after the game. Rumor had it that he was *very* well endowed.

"Wait here." I walked down to the front row and found a group of 6 nerdy looking dudes. "Hey boys," I said.

They all just stared at my tits. Which made sense, because the outfit I'd thrown together was amazing. I'd cut up a red Odegaard dress to turn it into a super low cut little crop top.

Eventually one of the guys tried to say something, but his voice caught in his throat.

"Mind if me and my friends sit here?"

He nodded and pushed his friends down the bench. But it wasn't nearly enough room. Scooter alone wouldn't have even fit on the little bit of bench they'd vacated.

"Could you guys actually just move somewhere else? If you do, I'll text you a pic of my boobs later."

I'd never seen someone get out of their seat so quickly. For a second they even forgot to give me a phone number to send my boob pic to, but then one of them sprinted back down the stairs and gave me a little slip of paper with a number written on it.

I waved for everyone to come and join me.

"Wow," said Chad. "How'd you get those guys to move?"

"You offer blowjob?" asked Slavanka, miming a blow-job.

Chad shot her a look. "She better not have. Or some nerds are gonna get their asses beat."

"Relax, babe. I'm not gonna blow any nerds today." *A football player, though? Maybe.* I looked down at the field to see if the rumors about the quarterback were true, but Harvard's defense was on the field. And they sucked, so no blowjobs for them. Seriously - they'd already let Cornell score 35 points. And by the looks of it…they were probably going to give up another touchdown after that last catch gained 20 yards. Seriously…that guy had been wide open!

"Don't turn around," said a gruff voice behind us.

I turned around to see who the sexy voice belonged to. But he wasn't sexy. Or at least…I couldn't tell if he was sexy or not. Because he was disguised as the Harvard mascot, John the Pilgrim, complete with an oversized foam mask and a big maroon tricorn.

He turned his permanently smiling head to check me out, and then he turned his focus back to Chad and his friends. "I'm going to ask you three a series of questions about Harvard. If I don't hear the correct answer within ten seconds, then you need not show up to the Gryphon Club party this evening. Or ever. Understood?"

The boys all nodded without looking back.

"When was Harvard founded?" asked the mascot.

"1636," said Chad.

"How many Nobel laureates are associated with Harvard?"

"160."

"Presidents?"

"Eight."

The quiz went on and on forever. Chad knew most of the answers. And whenever he didn't know one, Trent would chime in. Together, they were flawless with their Harvard trivia.

How long is this gonna go on? We'd gotten to the game near the end of the third quarter, and now it was well into the fourth. More importantly, I needed a hot dog. And I couldn't send Chad to fetch me one until he was finished with his little quiz.

"What is the significance of the three headed monster?" asked the mascot.

Chad shifted in his seat. "The three headed monster is, uh…"

"Significant because…" added Trent.

Oh come on, guys! How had they not heard about the three headed monster? *The Towel Drop* was posting like an article a day about it. And it was all anyone could talk about on the *Hot Football Studs* forum.

I thought Scooter might finally be able to help out with an answer, but he stayed silent. Their ten seconds were almost up.

Good thing they brought me.

"The three headed monster refers to three true freshmen on the Harvard football team," I said to the mascot. "And they're significant because they're all projected to go in the top 10 of the NFL draft when they achieve eligibility at the end of their junior year. That will be the first time any Harvard player has gone in the first round." They were also significant because they were extremely hot. I couldn't wait for them to get on the field again so I could keep checking them out.

"Correct," said the mascot. "And who are you?"

I turned in my chair to look at him again. "I'm Chastity Morgan. And I'm significant because…well, look at me. But since you seem to be mostly concerned with career accomplishments, I'm also significant because I'm going to turn Daddy's real estate empire into the world's first trillion-dollar business."

"I didn't ask why you were significant."

"I know."

"I was asking who you are because you weren't the one supposed to be answering my questions. This was a test for potential brothers of the Gryphon Club. Which they have now failed."

"Wrong," I corrected. "You said that you needed to hear an answer to each question within 10 seconds. You never specified *who* had to give the answer."

He let out a heavy sigh. "Very well. One final question. Who are the three heads of the three headed monster?"

"Easy," I replied. "Running back Shaka Hung, wide receiver Flash Robinson, and quarterback Adonis Papachristodoulopoulos."

The mascot listened very carefully as I said each syllable of Adonis' last name. But I said it flawlessly, because I'm awesome. And it didn't hurt that I'd typed it like a billion times while google image searching him to try to find some proper dick pics.

"Not bad," said the mascot. He handed a piece of paper labeled PASSWORD to Chad and then got up and left.

Chad let out a huge sigh, like he'd been holding his breath the entire time they were being quizzed. "Oh my God. I thought we were screwed when he asked about the three headed monster."

"Luckily you have the most amazing girlfriend ever," I said. "And to thank me for my amazingness, I'll take one hot dog please. Actually, make it two. Have I told you my theory that meat and bread go straight to my tits?"

Trent looked at my boobs. "You must have been eating a lot of meat and bread then."

Damn right I have. I pushed my arms together to make my cleavage look even more amazing.

Chad punched him in the arm. "Dude, stop looking at her tits. Come on, let's go get some hot dogs."

Ash and Slavanka put their orders in and then the boys got up to get our snacks.

"Alright, ladies," I said. "The offense is finally coming onto the field. This is our chance to get noticed by the players." I slid a big foam finger onto my hand and then stood up to cheer. "Go Harvard!" I yelled, jumping up and down.

"Ahh!" yelled Ash. "Be careful!" She grabbed my arm and yanked me back onto the bench.

"What?" I asked.

She pointed to my chest. "Your boob was popping out!"

"No, no," said Slavanka. "Tasteful underboob." She honked my boobs twice to properly compliment my outfit, a la Single Girl Rule #20.

"Aw, thanks girl. I agree, my underboob was quite tasteful. And if the players wanna see more, they're gonna have to invite me to their locker room to help celebrate their victory."

"Is that really a thing that happens?" asked Ash.

"Uh, of course it is. Most of the confirmed sightings on *The Towel Drop* are from girls who got invited back into the locker room to be the post-game entertainment."

Ash's eyes got huge. "And by post-game entertainment, you mean…a gangbang?"

"Oh my God, Ash! You're so naughty. Of course they don't get gangbanged. They usually just blow the MVP of the game. But it's not unheard of for a few other guys to join in if they have really big cocks. So yeah, I guess sometimes it's a gangbang."

"Please tell me you're not going to leave us alone with Chad and his friends. Scooter keeps telling me about his workout routine and I don't know how to tell him to stop."

"Of course I'm not going to leave you alone! I'm thinking that Single Girl Rule #3 is actually: Never let a friend go into a *locker room* alone. So you and Slavanka can definitely come with me. Together we can try to tame the three-headed monster. Which one do you want? I've got my eye on Adonis, but the other two definitely look interesting. Maybe we should all just take turns with each of them?"

Ash started breathing really fast. "Tame a monster? Why would you think I'm into monster erotica? Did you see something on my phone? Not that there's anything to see. Okay! Fine! I admit it. I read an article about a big-foot sex book being really popular so I downloaded a sample. But it was weird. There was so much foot stuff. And his feet were so big." She fanned her armpits.

Is she nervous or turned on? "Whoa, relax. We're not gonna bang a literal monster. It's the three headed monster."

"I'm so confused."

"The three headed monster! They're literally all anyone can talk about on *The Towel Drop*." How has no one heard about this but me?

"The towel what?" asked Ash.

"Hold everything. You've never heard of *The Towel Drop*?"

Ash shook her head.

"Wow. Seriously?" Then it hit me. "I guess you prefer *The Daily Bulge*?"

"You mean *The Daily Bugle?* Like in Spiderman?"

I laughed. But it didn't seem like she was joking. Which meant she was majorly missing out on some delicious man candy. "Okay, wow. You have a lot of catching up to do. But luckily I'm here to bring you up to speed on all the hot goss about the three headed monster." I looked down at the field. Harvard's offense was driving. "The first part of the three headed monster is Shaka Hung, the running back. Known colloquially as Master Hung due to his patient, almost meditative running style." Right on cue, he took a handoff and came to nearly a complete stop behind the offensive line. A linebacker broke through and tried to tackle him, but Master Hung effortlessly stepped aside and the would-be tackler came up empty. Then a hole opened up and Hung absolutely *exploded* into it. He juked out two more defenders before someone finally latched onto him. But they *still* couldn't take him down. He must have had ridiculous balance, because it took three defenders literally riding on his back to bring him down.

"HUNNNNG!" chanted the crowd.

"He's actually pretty impressive," said Ash.

I squinted to try to get a better look. "You can see his bulge from here? I guess he's your pick, then?"

"I was talking about the run! And just because I read half of one weird book, it doesn't mean I'm a sex freak. I'm a good girl. So no gangbangs for me."

So now we're pretending like last night never happened? And when did a sample become half the book? Interesting… "Technically it will be an orgy if three of us are with three guys."

Ash looked around and then shushed me. "Can you be a little quieter? I think people are starting to stare. And anyway…you're here with your fiancé!"

"Correction…boyfriend. And what's your point? Single Girl Rule #8 is still in effect. And according to *The Towel*

Drop's patented bulge analysis technology, Master Hung is at least 8 inches."

"No, no," said Slavanka. "Asian penis small."

"I thought that was just a myth," said Ash.

"Not according to science. One study I saw found that the average guy from Congo is 7.1 inches. While the average in China is only 4.2 inches. Honestly, both of those are a little sad. But at least 7.1 inches is a better starting point."

"So Master Hung has a little baby penis then?" asked Ash. "I think *The Towel Drop* may need to recalibrate their bulge analyzer."

"Nope. He's half black and half Asian. Could you really not tell that from his last run? The man has the focus of a Buddhist monk combined with the sheer physical dominance of a Zulu warlord."

"Wow, yeah. I don't know how I missed that," said Ash. "Seriously though…this is all made up, right? There can't really be a website called *The Towel Drop* that's all about football players' dicks."

Where did sassy Ash come from all of a sudden? Maybe she was getting dehydrated from sweating so much thinking about what these big strong football players were gonna do to us.

I grabbed my phone and pulled up *The Towel Drop*. I scrolled down a bit to the article titled: "Is Master Hung really hung?"

I was gonna pass my phone to her, but the crowd started cheering. I looked up just in time to see Master Hung jump clean over a defender and then plow through another into the endzone.

I jumped up from my seat, cheering like a wild woman. There was no way he'd be able to ignore my underboob.

He glanced over at me for a second, but then he got swarmed by his teammates.

"Okay. I admit, that jump was pretty hot," said Ash.

"So you're in for the orgy?"

"No!"

"Oh, I know what's going on. You want all of them for yourself. You're trying to tackle Single Girl Rule #28: All girls should try at least one threesome. I'll be honest, Ash, I'm not sure you're ready for that rule yet. It's farther down on the list for a reason."

"I'm not invoking Single Girl Rule #28. I don't want that. I don't even want it with just Master Hung. He's way too thick for my taste."

"Too thick? What does that even mean? Also…what makes you think his cock is so thick?" I tilted my head to try to see what she was seeing.

"I was talking about his thighs. Look at those things! They're like…each the size of my torso."

"Yeah they are. *The Towel Drop* doesn't reveal what metrics go into their bulge analyzer, but I've been suspecting for a while that thigh size might indicate a nice girthy cock."

"That's a real shame," said Ash. "If it were long and thin then I'd totally be in."

Ooh. Sassy Ash had suddenly turned into horny Ash. I was wondering when that little sip of banana juice she'd taken would kick in. "Then I have just the man for you. Ash, meet Flash Robinson. Part two of the three headed monster." I pointed to Flash. And when Ash looked at him, her jaw literally dropped. Because unlike Master Hung…Flash's penis size wasn't a mystery.

"It's like he's smuggling a water bottle in his pants," whispered Ash.

I nodded. "It's not exactly thin. But it's definitely long like you requested."

"What's long?" asked Chad. He handed me two plain hotdogs - just meat and bread. My tits were gonna love these.

"Nothing," said Ash. "Nothing is long. I mean, I'm sure *someone's* penis is long. But that wasn't what I was requesting to be long. I just wanted a nice, long…"

"Hot dog," I said. I picked one up out of the bun and slapped Ash in the face with it.

"Oh God," she said, trying to dodge it. "It's so long. Just like I requested."

"Okay…" Chad sat down and started eating his own hot dog.

Scooter shoved four hamburger patties into his mouth and washed it down with a protein shake. "What'd we miss?"

"Harvard just got a touchdown," I said. "So now they're only down by one score."

"One score is 5 points?" asked Slavanka.

I turned to her. "Have you never watched football before?"

"We no have football. Only slap fight."

"Slap fight?" I asked.

"Yes, yes. Slap fight. Drink vodka, then take turns slap. Loser is first one to fall over or cry like little bitch boy." She pointed right at Chad when she said *little bitch boy*.

"Hey, why are you pointing at me?" asked Chad.

"Actually, I lie. One time we play soccer with Comrade Grigory head."

"Is that really what you guys call a soccer ball?" asked Ash. "Kinda like we call a football a pig skin?"

"No, no. One time Comrade Grigory plant wrong crop. So he lose head." She dragged her thumb across her neck. "Whole village play soccer and have much fun." She looked so happy about the memory.

"I have so many questions," said Chad. But he never got to ask them, because Harvard just recovered an onside kick. The whole stadium went nuts. The three headed monster had the ball again. All they had to do was drive down the field and score.

And then they could take me and my girls back to the locker room and have their way with us. I knew Ash hadn't technically said yes yet, but her reaction to Flash's bulge had said it all.

I still had to get their attention, though.

Flashing them would be the easiest way, of course. But I didn't want Chad to get mad and embarrass himself in front of the coolest guys on campus. No…I needed a more subtle way to get their attention. I took a bite of my hot dog while I thought about a solution.

And then it hit me.

The hot dogs!

I waited for a cameraman to be looking in our general direction, and then I grabbed a hotdog in each of my fists and licked them seductively.

"Oh my God!" said Ash, pointing up at the scoreboard. "We're on the jumbotron! Do I have food on my face? Oh no…" She stared dabbing her completely clean face with a napkin.

I shoved one of the hotdogs into my mouth, inch by inch, until it was jammed into my throat. And then slapped my face with the other.

A whistle blew.

"Delay of game, offense, #9," announced the ref.

"Damn it, Adonis!" yelled Harvard's coach. "Quit checking out the fans!"

I smiled to myself. *Mission accomplished.* Not only had Adonis noticed me, but he'd been so distracted by my little performance that he'd totally forgotten about the game.

Adonis. He was the third head of the three headed monster. And probably the hottest. He was 6'6 of pure muscle. But it wasn't just his body that made people refer to him as a god amongst boys. What really earned him that nickname was that he was always one step ahead of the defense. He was just smarter than everyone else on the field. He was basically the male version of me.

Except when he was being distracted by me.

There were only 5 seconds left in the game. Enough time for one play. And they were still about 60 yards away from scoring.

So I stopped eating my hotdogs seductively and let him focus.

Adonis dropped back to pass. I thought he was gonna get sacked, but he stiff-armed the defender right in the face. I almost felt bad for the defender. But not really...because all I could think about was how fun it would be to have Adonis shove something stiff in my face after the game.

He shook off one more defender and then hurled a bomb fifty yards downfield to Flash Robinson.

Flash caught it in stride. There were no defenders even close to him thanks to his blinding speed, but he still caught it with one hand just to show off. He did a few high steps and then backflipped into the endzone to end the game.

The crowd went nuts, and Flash was loving every second of it. He tore off his helmet and posed for the camera, making sure to turn so that everyone could see the lightning bolts shaved into the sides of his hair.

"I hope you're ready for a wild time," I whispered to Ash. It may have been traditional for the player of the game to get a nice post-game blowjob, but there was no way Flash would stop there. He was definitely gonna make a huge show of fucking Ash in every position imaginable.

"No! No, no, no!" she hissed back. "You haven't even gotten an invite yet."

"Just wait for it." I looked down at the field and locked eyes with Adonis. He'd taken the game-winning ball from Flash and was headed my way. And he got more and more handsome with every step he took. It wasn't even fair for someone to be that handsome *and* that talented. A few people online speculated that he couldn't possibly have a huge dick too, but I didn't subscribe to that theory. There was no preset limit on how much awesomeness one person could have. Take me, for example. I was amazing in every way.

Adonis wrote something on the ball with a sharpy and tossed it up to me with a big smile.

Yes! As the ball spun through the air, I could see that he'd signed it and added his phone number. The number I needed to call to get my locker room invitation.

I was about to grab it, but Chad snatched it out of the air.

"Dude! Thanks!" yelled Chad.

"Hey! That was for me." I reached for the ball, but Chad pulled back.

"No way. Why would he give it to you?"

"Uh…because I'm the hottest girl here." *Duh.* "Why would he give it to *you?*"

"Because he thinks I'm awesome. I've talked to him a few times in line at the dining hall. We were totally vibing."

"Dude, Adonis has no idea who you are," said Trent.

"Of course he does. I'm pretty sure that my witty banter with him is what got us invited to the party tonight."

"Uh, no. Sorry, that was obviously my dad. Senator Kenneth Donahue."

"Yeah, I know who your dad is. And it was probably a combo. I mean…Adonis' balls don't lie." Chad held up the ball with a huge smile on his face. "Look, it even has his phone number."

"I bet you'd like Adonis' balls in your mouth," said Scooter. "Race you back to the dorms. Last one back has to lick Adonis' ball." He jumped over two rows of seats and sprinted for the exit, pushing about a dozen people over in the process.

Trent and Chad sprinted off behind him. Carrying *my* football.

"He take gangbang invite?" asked Slavanka.

"Yeah," I said with a sigh. I looked back at the field to see if Adonis was still out there, but the teams had already headed to the locker rooms. I'd missed my chance. For now. "Come on, girls. Let's go get ready for this party tonight. There's no way Adonis isn't a member of the Gryphon Club…which means there will be plenty of opportunities for me to properly show him that Chad has the hottest girlfriend. And by that I mean I'm gonna suck his cock."

Chapter 6

GENERAL ORVILLE THUNDERSTICK III
Saturday, Sept 14, 2013

We left the stadium just in time to see Scooter and Trent jump into Scooter's Lambo and speed off.

"I wonder how he can even see with the windshield cracked like that," said Ash.

Apparently the answer was that he couldn't, because he went from 0 to 60 in about 3 seconds flat and crashed directly into a lamp post that had been in front of him the entire time.

Then it was a whole big scene.

An ambulance came. Trent got stretchered away. Blah blah blah. None of the paramedics were hot, so I didn't really pay much attention to what was happening.

Long story short, Trent would be in the hospital all night, so he couldn't come to the party. We'd had to walk back to their dorm, and now we were running late. And Ash was freaking out.

"Don't worry," said Scooter. He tried to put his arm around Ash, but she squirmed away. "I'll get us there in no time."

"No way," said Chad.

"Why? Oh. You're worried that I'll crash again?"

"Yes."

"Well, that's dumb. What are the odds that I'd total two Lambos in one day?"

"For a guy who's nicknamed Scooter because you crashed three scooters in 12 hours, I'd say pretty high."

Scooter grunted. "You're missing some important context there."

"Am I?" asked Chad. "Am I really?"

Scooter adjusted his pink bowtie and mumbled the saddest little, "No."

"I really think it's best if we just don't go," said Ash. She looked longingly at the big screen TV that took up nearly an entire wall of Chad's dorm room. "Anyone up for a *Parks and Rec* marathon?"

"And miss the party of the year?" I asked. "No way!"

"But…"

"I'll watch TV with you every night this week if you come," I said. I wasn't able to leave her side until I figured out the true meaning of Rule #3 anyway, so I was gonna be hanging with her every night.

"Hmm…deal. But only if I can wear my comfy sneakers!"

I looked down at her feet. Heels would have looked better, but her sneakers weren't the worst. They were somewhere in the middle. Not worthy of a boob honking, but also not bad enough to invoke Single Girl Rule #17: Friends don't let friends wear ugly outfits. #RealTalk. "Deal." We shook on it and then Ghostie picked us up and drove us to the Gryphon Club.

The frat houses at the University of New Castle were charming in their own way, but they were pretty much just old colonial Victorian houses with a few Greek letters thrown on the front. The Gryphon Club, on the other hand, owned an entire estate. Right in the middle of downtown Cambridge. It was so fancy that you couldn't even see it from the road.

The gate swung open automatically as Ghostie turned onto the driveway. And then we had to drive another three minutes up a twisty, tree-lined drive.

Eventually we got to one of the coolest mansions I'd ever seen. And that was saying something. Because Daddy owned a lot of mansions. But his were mostly sleek and modern. The Gryphon Club, on the other hand, was in a freaking gothic castle.

"Ahh!" I squealed. "This is gonna be so much fun. I love castle parties."

"Are you sure this is the right place?" asked Ash. "It kinda looks like somewhere you'd go if you wanted to get murdered."

"Check out the grotesques." I pointed to the roof.

"The what?" asked Ash.

"She's talking about the gargoyles," said Chad.

"Oh. Are those supposed to make me feel better? Because those things are creepy as hell."

"Look closer," I said.

Ash pressed her face to the glass. "Ah, I see it. They look like gryphons."

"Do they?" I tilted my head. "Huh. I guess they do."

"Wait, what were you talking about?"

"Their dicks, of course. Look at those things!" I tilted my head. "If I'm not mistaken, that's the work of the one and only Leopold van Doren." He was my all-time favorite grotesque sculptor, because unlike most, he understood that grotesques were just a way to put penis sculptures on churches without getting in trouble.

Ash's eyes got big.

"Yes, yes. Van Doren sculpt best penis," said Slavanka.

"No way!" I said. "Are you a fellow grotesque connoisseur?" Slavanka just kept getting cooler and cooler.

"What about penises?" asked Scooter.

I pointed up at the roof.

"Well shit," he said. "I'm gonna have to sue the Gryphon Club, because they were not authorized to use the likeness of my dick on their gargoyles."

Yeah right.

"I think maybe I'll just have Ghost take me back to the dorms…" said Ash.

"I'll go back with you," said Scooter. "I can make you an octuple-egg smoothie and we can try out some new BFR bands I got. What do you squat? 450?"

"Uh, actually. I already promised Chastity that I'd go to this party." Ash got out of the limo so fast.

Thank you, Scooter.

We all followed her up to the front door. I grabbed the eagle head knocker and tapped it against the thick wooden door.

A little window slid open and two dark eyes peered through at us. "Password?"

I stepped aside to let Chad answer.

"Roses are red, violets are blue. For my future brothers, I brought something new." He gestured to me, Ash, and Slavanka.

Oooh. I'm their offering? Yes, please.

The window slammed shut and then the door creaked open. But no one was there. It was just a dimly lit foyer with way too much wood trim on the walls.

"I guess we go in?" asked Chad.

I shrugged and stepped inside. Everyone else followed. And then the door slammed shut behind us.

Ash jumped and grabbed my arm.

"It's okay," I said. "They're just messing with us. Classic pledge hazing."

"Is it?" asked Ash. "I really think we're about to get murdered."

"We'll protect you," said Chad, puffing out his chest.

Slavanka laughed. "Hehe. Friendboy make funny joke." She pried a great sword out of the hands of one of the suits or armor that lined the hallway. "Now we safe."

We took a few more steps into the hallway. And then Ash tapped my shoulder. "Pssst. Chastity."

"Yeah?"

"I have to pee. Like…really badly. Scary things shrink my bladder."

"Okay, we'll find you a bathroom. Wait a second! This must be what Single Girl Rule #3 is all about. Never let your friend go into a bathroom alone *in a creepy mansion.*"

"Sure," said Ash, jumping back and forth with her legs pressed together. "Just find me a bathroom before I pee my pants."

"I got you." I turned to Chad and Scooter. "We'll be right back. Ash has to pee."

"You can't just leave us," said Chad. "The invitation was very specific. We were supposed to bring girls."

"Okay. Slavanka will stay with you guys. I'll go with Ash."

"Actually," said Ash. "I'd prefer if Slavanka went with me. You know…since she has a sword and all."

I shrugged. "As long as you don't have to go alone, then the Single Girl Rules are satisfied."

Slavanka and Ash ran off.

"What now?" asked Chad.

And to answer his question, a door opened.

A cloaked figure emerged. "Good evening, gentlemen. Thank you for coming. And for bringing such a beautiful offering. Please join us." He stepped aside and gestured into the room. A dozen or so cloaked figures were inside, all lounging on plush sofas talking to girls in party dresses. I craned my neck to see if Adonis was one of the guys. The cloaks made it difficult to be sure, but none of them looked quite tall enough to be him.

Chad started to walk in, but the cloaked man put his arm up to bar his entry. "Not you. I was talking to her."

"Huh?" asked Chad. "Then what are we supposed to do?"

He pointed down the hallway. "Go down the hall and take a left. Door 3A."

"So you want us to go into some weird room while you party with my girl?"

"The company you keep reveals a great deal about your character. Now please, let's not waste any more time. You're already one of the last to arrive." He gestured again for me to enter the room.

So I was supposed to go flirt with the members of the Gryphon Club while Chad got hazed? *Hmmm…*

"No thanks," I said. "Door 3A sounds more fun." I booped him on his masked nose and then hooked arms with Chad and Scooter. We walked off down the hall while the cloaked figure surely gaped at me. And definitely stared at my ass. Because this dress hugged me in all the right places.

"Are you sure that was the right move?" whispered Chad.

"Yeah. Think about it. The Gryphon Club wants grown ass men. Not little bitches who are willing to let them flirt with their girls. The only thing they'll be able to talk about all night is the smoke show in the little red dress who didn't want to hang with them."

"Shit, you're right," said Chad.

"I know." I opened door 3A and we walked into an antechamber with a table right in the center. Little notecards sat on silver trays. It was like name cards at a wedding. Only instead of names, these just had numbers. And we must have been awfully late to the party, because only three remained. The sign in the middle of the table instructed us to "TAKE ONE, LEAVE YOUR PHONE, AND GO TO YOUR PLACE."

The only three numbers left were 22, 23, and 24.

Hmmm… Single Girl Rule #23: Never back down from a huge cock. #Fearless. The first part of that didn't apply here (unless this hazing was about to get *very* interesting), but the #Fearless definitely did. So I grabbed 23.

Chad took 22, and Scooter took 24. We put our phones in a big bowl and then joined the rest of the pledges in the main room. The light was so dim that it was hard to make out much, but it appeared to be a library that had been stripped of all furniture. The only thing that remained were floor-to-ceiling mahogany bookshelves, a ton of books, and a number of old marble busts.

No, not just any number of busts. There were 24 of them. And each one was wearing a gold medallion with a number on it. The only three without someone standing in front of them were the three numbers we'd just grabbed.

I walked over to #23, and as I got closer, I was sure I'd made the right choice. Because while most of the busts were of wrinkly old men, #23 was a total stud. Based on his twirly mustache and mutton chops, I guessed he'd been dead for at least 150 years. But back in his day, I bet that dude *fucked.*

"Good evening," boomed a voice.

"Holy shit," hissed Chad, jumping and clutching my arm.

I patted his hand to calm him. There was nothing to be afraid of. The five cloaked figures that had appeared on the far side of the library weren't even carrying and swords or ropes or anything. Although I was quite curious about how they had appeared there. Because there were no doors on that side of the library…

One of the cloaked men stepped forward. "Welcome to the most important night of your lives. Four teams will set out tonight. But only one will return victorious."

He stepped back and another cloaked man stepped forward. I wasn't really sure why...maybe the first guy could only remember those three lines? Either way, it made for a nice dramatic effect.

"The winning team will be one step closer to joining the most exclusive brotherhood ever created. The rest of you will be exposed as the worthless peasants that you are. Fail tonight, and membership in the Gryphon Club will be forever out of your grasp."

He stepped back into the row of cloaked figures. A third stepped forward.

"Each of you is standing in front of a bust immortalizing the very best that Harvard has to offer. To honor those alumni, you will each be given a task that you must perform without question or complaint until the day you are initiated."

The fourth cloaked figure stepped out of the line and walked over to the guy standing by statue #1.

"Pledge #1," he yelled, which was totally unnecessary since he was standing like 2 feet away from him. "Which Harvard alum do you honor?"

Once he recovered from the super aggressive yelling, Pledge #1 turned and read the placard beneath his statue. "I honor Henry T. Walker, sir."

"Correct!" yelled the cloaked guy. "And to honor the true inventor of blue jeans, you shall wear the same pair of jeans every day. And every Sunday, we'll cut two inches of material off until you're wearing the sassiest little pair of daisy dukes that this campus has ever seen. Do I make myself clear?"

"Sir, yes sir!" Pledge #1 gave a salute, which felt appropriate based on the drill sergeant vibes of the cloaked guy.

"Let's see how they fit!" The drill sergeant grabbed a wrapped present next to the statue and handed it to Pledge #1. He pulled his pants off and slid into his new jeans. They were even tighter than I'd expected them to be. And the poor guy didn't even have a nice package to fill them out. Something told me that he would not be a future member of the Gryphon Club.

The cloaked figure moved on to Pledge #2, who announced he was honoring a star basketball player.

"Correct! And to honor him, you'll dribble a basketball everywhere you go. If anyone asks why, you'll tell them that you're doing it, 'For the love of the game.' "

Pledge #2 laughed. "This is bullshit. I'm not doing that."

I thought the drill sergeant was gonna go ballistic on him, but he stayed perfectly calm. In fact, he didn't even respond.

The bookshelf behind Pledge #2 swung open and four gloved hands yanked him backwards. It happened so fast that he didn't even have time to scream. I blinked and the bookshelf was whole again, with Pledge #2 nowhere to be seen.

I made a mental note to tell Daddy to have something like that installed in our library. That was a badass way to deal with annoying idiots.

The drill sergeant moved to Pledge #3, who eagerly agreed to act as the Gryphon Club's 24/7 on-call tech support in honor of tech mogul James Hunter.

James Hunter is a member of the Gryphon Club? Now I *really* wanted to help Chad get in. Because rumor had it that James had a huge dick. And that he knew how to use it.

If Chad could get close to him, then maybe I could find out if those rumors were true.

The rest of the pledges all agreed to ridiculous things as well...but all I could focus on was trying to figure out what I was gonna have to do. I had a feeling I was going to end up with a mustache and mutton chops. Which wouldn't be the best look for me, but I guess I had the bone structure to pull it off. Ooooh! Maybe I'd have to go around asking random guys for mustache rides. Now *that* would be a fun mission.

"And who are you honoring?" demanded the drill sergeant. He was even louder now that he was standing in front of Chad, only a few feet to my right.

Chad totally butchered some Asian prince's name.

"That's the father of modern medicine in Thailand, you worthless idiot! And to honor him, you'll address every person of authority as 'Daddy' for the rest of the semester. Including all members of the Gryphon Club. Do I make myself clear, son?"

"Yes, Daddy!" shouted Chad.

I stifled a laugh. The way he said it sounded so sexual.

The drill sergeant came to me next. "Who are you honoring?" It didn't really seem like he was looking at me. He was looking past me at my statue, probably trying to remember whatever crazy task I was going to be assigned.

I turned and read the plaque of my handsome mustachioed bust. "I'm honoring General Orville Thunderstick III, sir."

"General Thunderstick once killed a dozen confederate soldiers bare-ass naked using his underwear as his only weapon. So to honor him, you shall go commando for the rest of the semester."

I needed so much more information about why he was naked and how he killed twelve men using only his underwear. But I'd have to research that on my own time.

"Yes sir," I said. I reached up my skirt, pulled my thong off, and handed it to the drill sergeant.

He got a weird look on his face and looked down at his hand.

"Why the fuck were you wearing a lacy thong?" he yelled. And then he finally looked at me. "And why are you dressed like a lady?"

"Because I am a lady." I pushed my tits up for him.

"Women aren't allowed in the Gryphon Club."

"And yet here I am, at the Gryphon Club, receiving pledge instructions. But if you want to give me my thong back..." I reached for it, but he pulled his hand away. "Does that mean I can stay?"

"For now."

That's what I thought.

He moved on to Scooter, who would be honoring Teddy Roosevelt's famous foreign policy of "Speak softly but carry a big stick," by only whispering for the rest of the semester and also carrying a 6-foot walking stick around everywhere he went.

Scooter whispering everything would be entertaining, but I still liked Chad's the most.

The drill sergeant returned to the line of cloaked figures and the fifth one stepped forward.

"We take honoring these great men very seriously. If you see a fellow pledge violating his assignment, please report it immediately. Failure to report will be viewed as collusion."

"Understood?!" boomed the drill sergeant.

"Yes, sir!" we all agreed. Except for Chad, who yelled, "Yes, Daddy!"

"Then let the games begin." The wall behind cloaked figures opened and they all walked through it. But it didn't close behind them. Whatever the games were, I had a feeling they started through those doors.

YES, DADDY
Saturday, Sept 14, 2013

We walked through the secret doors into an office. Some digital cameras and four sheets of paper were waiting for us on the desk, each labeled with a range of 6 numbers. I picked up the paper for "Team D - 19 to 24" and started reading:

Gryphon Club Scavenger Hunt
Tonight your team must get pictures of every item on this list. The first team to complete the hunt and return to the Gryphon Club wins. All other teams will be eliminated from consideration.

1. A gryphon statue
2. A dildo from a sorority
3. An authentic samurai helmet
4. The John Harvard statue
5. A sports car worth more than $100K
6. Posing in a store display window
7. Dancing in the library
8. A topless girl
9. One of you getting a piggyback ride from the captain of the football team
10. Something heinous
Good luck!

P.S. Every member of your team must appear in every picture.

P.P.S. Every picture must also feature one of you wearing a thong and holding two cucumbers.

"Ah!" I squealed. "This is gonna be so much fun!" I grabbed the list and a camera off the desk. "Let's go!"

We ran out of the mansion.

"Wait!" said Chad as we ran past one of the gryphon shaped grotesques. "We need a picture with one of these."

"Yeah, but it won't do us any good until one of us is in a thong holding two cucumbers."

"Shit, I forgot about that. It's gonna take so long to go get that stuff and then come back here."

"It would. But there's nothing on the rules that says the pictures have to be taken in order."

"You're a genius," said Chad.

"I know!" I gave him a kissy face. "I almost have our path all planned out. Just need to google something real quick…"

I pulled my backup phone out of my purse.

"Hey," said one of our teammates. I hadn't been paying attention when he'd been assigned his pledge mission, but I had a feeling it had something to do with the watermelon he was carrying. "I thought we were supposed to leave our phones when we took our numbers?"

"That's her backup phone," said Chad.

"Her what?"

I ignored them and shot off a few texts, including one to Ash and Slavanka telling them to get their butts outside to the front lawn. Then I googled museums nearby. There was one not far from here with a samurai helmet on display. I looked down the list one more time just to make sure I had everything accounted for.

"Alright guys," I said. "We can do this entire hunt in only three stops. I'll have us back here in less than two hours."

One of our other teammates gasped. "My lady! That of which you speak dost be most impossible."

Say what? I stared at him.

He shrugged and held up a book filled with Shakespeare plays. If he was supposed to be talking like he was permanently in a Shakespeare play, then he was failing miserably. Had he never heard of iambic pentameter?

"Don't doubt her," said Chad. "Like I said, she's a genius."

"But how?" whispered Scooter. He took the list from me and looked down it. "It will take at least two hours just to walk from here to a sorority house to Harvard Yard to the football stadium."

"Football stadium?"

"Yeah," said Chad. "They have a few statues of some former Harvard captains. It's pretty common for students to jump up onto their shoulders and take piggyback rides while tailgating."

"We're not walking. And we're not going to the stadium." Did these basic bitches not remember that Adonis - quarterback and captain of the football team - had given us his phone number on the signed ball? "Ah, perfect timing."

Ash and Slavanka ran out of the mansion just as Ghostie pulled up in a limo. We all piled in.

"Take us to a sorority house," I said.

He grunted a response, which in Ghostie-speak meant…yes.

"Can you drop us off at the dorms first?" asked Ash. "Almost getting murdered really tuckered me out."

"We find murder room," agreed Slavanka.

"Murder room?" I asked.

Ash nodded. The look on her face made me think that this so-called "murder room" was going to be haunting her dreams for quite some time. "We found the bathroom. And it was amazing. It was like the world's fanciest locker room. Like the kind you'd find at some country club for billionaires. But then we got lost. And we somehow ended up in the basement in a huge stone room. There was a gryphon-shaped throne on one end. And tons of melted candles around an altar. I'm pretty sure they do human sacrifice there."

"No way!" I said. "You found the legendary Gryphon Club sex altar."

Ash's eyes got even bigger. "Sex altar?"

"Yeah. Rumor has it that they use it to induct new members."

"Big gay gangbang?" asked Slavanka.

I laughed. "Maybe. But I'm pretty sure they watch new members bang girls. To build camaraderie."

"What girls?" asked Ash. "Did we just narrowly miss getting kidnapped and becoming the Gryphon Club's sex slaves? Wait! Why are we going to a sorority house? Please tell me that we haven't been tasked with finding new sex slaves for them."

"They don't have sex slaves," said Chad. "And we aren't doing any human trafficking tonight."

"*Tonight?*" asked Ash. "That kind of makes it seem like we're just putting the kidnapping off until tomorrow."

"Ash, no one is getting kidnapped tonight. Or ever." The Locatelli's had already tried to kidnap me once, and that hadn't worked very well. I doubted they'd be back. "Now give me your thong."

"What?" Ash's face started to turn red.

"I need your thong. Hand it over."

"I'm not…I don't wear those."

"Then what do you wear?"

"I prefer more coverage," she whispered. "Thongs are a breeding ground for bacteria. They touch *too* much."

Too much what? And what college girl didn't own a drawer of thongs? We really needed to go shopping. I turned to Slavanka. "I need your thong then."

"No thong."

"Slavanka, it's of the utmost importance."

"No thong. Underwear waste of money."

Seriously? What was wrong with my friends? It was like we were all in on honoring General Orville Thunderstick III. But no bother, I had a backup plan.

The limo pulled to a stop and we all got out in front of a rowhouse. A few Greek letters sat above the front door.

I rubbed my hands together. "Two cucumbers, a thong, and a dildo coming right up." I started to walk to the door, but Chad grabbed my arm.

"You got us a ride here," he said. "Now it's our turn to work our magic."

"Yeah," agreed Scooter. He turned to Chad. "Think you can reach that second-floor window if I give you a lift?"

Chad laughed. "There's no need to break in when you have a face like mine. Watch and learn." Chad strode up to the door with so much swagger.

Is he actually gonna pull this off? I got as close as I could without it being obvious that I was listening.

He rang the doorbell and some sorority girl answered. "Yes?"

"Hey," he said, casually leaning against the door jamb. "It's your lucky day."

She stared at him.

He pulled four tickets out of his pocket and fanned them out. "I've got four tickets to the biggest badminton match of the season. And if you play your cards right, they could be yours. Wanna know how?"

"No."

"To win, you just have to guess how big my cock is. I'll even give you three guesses. But you have to submit your guesses in the form of two cucumbers and a dildo. Oh, and I need one of your thongs too. As a way to remember who guessed what."

She slapped him and slammed the door shut.

"How'd it go?" I called to him.

He shook his head. "The girls here hate fun. Let's try a different sorority."

"Mind if I try?"

"Be my guest. But you're wasting your time. If I can't charm them, no one can."

Being charming was different than being pervy. My insignificant other sometimes acted so basic. I switched spots with Chad and rang the doorbell.

The same girl answered.

"Hey," I said. "I need your help."

"Oh God. Please tell me that pervert hasn't taken the streets to try to give out his lame badminton tickets."

I laughed. "What? No. I was just looking for…Jessica."

"Oh, okay. One sec." She ran off and started yelling for Jessica. It had been a bit of a gamble, but in high school I'd had at least 3 Jessicas in every class. There had to be at least one in this sorority. And apparently there was, because Jessica had just come to the door. Hopefully that other girl hadn't warned her about the badminton pervert looking for cucumbers and thongs.

"Hey, girl," I said. "I hate to bother you like this, but I was just out with my boyfriend at a party. We snuck up to a room to bang, and we were really going at it. But then his friends burst in and stole my thong and ran away. I threw my dress on and chased them all the way down the street, but they were too quick. So now here I am, standing in the middle of the city in the world's shortest dress with no panties on." I tugged on the hem of my dress, pretending to be uncomfortable about it. "Think you can help a girl out?"

"Wow," she said. "Guys can be such assholes. Come on in. I'm sure I can find you something." She took me up to her room and started rifling through some drawers. "How about some sweats?"

"I'd really prefer underwear. I don't want to do a walk of shame in sweats and this dress."

She snapped her fingers. "I have just the thing!" She went to a different drawer and pulled out a lacy red lingerie set with the tags still on. It looked hella cheap. "My ex-boyfriend got me this for Christmas. I was gonna wear it for him, but then he cheated on me."

"Aw, I'm sorry."

"Like I said, guys can be such assholes." She handed me the lingerie.

"I wish there was something we could to do get back at them. Like…what would my boyfriend do if I sent him a picture of me sucking a dick?"

"Oh my God. That would be epic."

"Have any realistic looking dildos?"

"Uh…" Jessica blushed.

"Girl, don't be ashamed. The bigger the better. I want to show him what a real man looks like."

She opened her desk drawer and pulled out an absolutely *massive* veiny black dildo.

"Oh, hell yeah!" I grabbed it from her. The thickness of it immediately conjured memories of last night at the banana party. It also made me wonder… *Is Adonis this big?* If all went according to plan, I'd find out soon enough. "My boyfriend is gonna flip when he gets a picture of my lips wrapped around this thing."

"You might wanna wash it first…"

"Good idea. Also…do you have any cucumbers? I'm so hungry for some dinner."

"Oh my God! You're on the cucumber diet too?"

Hell no. I didn't want my tits to shrivel up and die. I was on the meat and bread diet. But we didn't need meat and bread for the scavenger hunt. We needed cucumbers. "Yup. But I admit…I'm a bit of a cheater. I always eat two."

"Say no more. One cucumber is just not enough calories. I always try to buy the biggest ones."

"The bigger the better. But still two, please."

"You got it." She ran off and returned a second later with two cucumbers.

"You're a lifesaver." I balanced all my goodies in my hands and started down the stairs.

"Wait," said Jessica. "Aren't you gonna put them on?" She gestured to the lingerie.

I shook my head. "You've already been such a help. I don't want to impose any more than I already have. I'll change outside." I blew her a kiss and walked out the door. "Picture time!" I called to my team.

"What'd you say to her?" asked Chad.

"Just girl chat. Now, who's gonna wear the thong and hold the cucumbers for this first picture? I totes would, but I'm not allowed to wear underwear in honor of General Orville Thunderstick III." And even if I could, there was no way I'd be caught in *this* underwear. The tag said the entire set had only cost $300.

"I can't hold the cucumbers," whispered Scooter, holding up his six-foot walking stick.

"Me neither," said Watermelon.

I tried to hand Ash a cucumber but she swatted it out of my hand. "You know I'm scared of those!"

"Hey, I had to work hard for that!" I picked it up off the sidewalk. She was lucky it hadn't exploded.

I tucked the cucumbers under my arms to secure them as I held the lingerie out to Shakespeare.

He shook his head and opened to a page of his book. "The fault, dear Brutus, lies not within the thong, but in myself, that my underling is huge."

I stared at him, trying to process what the hell he'd just said. It sounded like a quote from Act 1 of Julius Caesar, but… *Ooooooh!* "Are you trying to tell us that your dick is far too big for this thong?"

He nodded.

Interesting. It was a shame he was ugly. And kinda dumb, based on his lack of knowledge of Shakespeare.

"I won't fit either," said Chad.

"Sure you will, babe." I tossed it to him.

"What about him?" He pointed to the last member of our team. The guy hadn't said anything yet, so I had no idea what his mission was. Maybe he wasn't allowed to talk?

"I'll go next," said the guy.

"Shouldn't we like rock-paper-scissors for it?" asked Chad.

"No time," I said. "Just put it on and let's get a picture with this sorority dildo." I tossed the thong to Chad and then tossed the rest of the set in the trash where it belonged.

He hid behind the trash can and slid into the lacy red thong.

"Well hot damn," he said, proudly stepping out from behind the trash can. "Who knew I'd look so good in a thong?" He struck a muscleman pose.

We all laughed. Except for Ash, who let out a little scream. "Take it off!" she whisper-yelled.

"Wow, Ash," I said. "Keep it in your pants. Chad is all mine."

"I meant for him to change back! Not to get full nude." She sounded frantic.

"Ignore the lace," said Chad in his sexiest voice. "Just look at these abs."

Just then a cop blared its siren a few times and pulled up to us.

Oooh. So that was why Ash was so scared. Speaking of Ash…where was she? I spun around looking for her. It didn't take long to spot her standing behind a tree that was no thicker than the dildo I was holding. But when she realized I could see her, she got down and started army crawling along the grass to find a new hiding spot.

The cop got out of his car and approached Chad. "Good evening, sir. Can I see some ID please?"

"Sure. Can you hold this?" He handed a cucumber to the cop and backed over to his pile of clothes behind the trashcans, being careful not to moon the officer. Then he fished his wallet out of his pants and handed his ID over. The officer took it back to his squad car to search for outstanding warrants.

"I think you're forgetting something, *son,*" whispered Scooter to Chad.

"Cowards die many times before their deaths," said Shakespeare. "The valiant never taste of death but once." He looked so pleased with himself for actually using a quote pretty well.

"Nah, I'm not scared to do my mission," said Chad. "I'm just waiting for the right moment."

"Better be," said Watermelon. "Otherwise we'll have to report you."

The cop came back out and handed Chad his ID back. "Mr. Chadwick. Are you aware that public indecency is a crime?"

"Yes, Daddy," said Chad.

The cop cleared his throat. "Did you just call me Daddy?"

"That depends. Do you want me to call you Daddy? Or are you gonna have to punish me?" He put his hands on the trashcan and presented his bare ass to the cop.

"I'm not with them!" screamed Ash as she took off running down the street.

Her instinct seemed pretty spot on. I was pretty sure Chad was totally fucked. And he'd never looked hotter. His penis may have fit in a women's size small thong, but his balls must have been the size of fucking coconuts for him to talk to the cop like that.

There was a long pause as the cop processed everything he was seeing. And then he shook his head. "Sir, please accept my sincerest apology. I thought you were some douchey frat guy dressed like an idiot. But now I can see that you're just being authentically you. And I'm so proud of you for that. Don't ever let anyone tell you how you should dress just because of the equipment you were born with. And if any frat guys ever give you any trouble, don't hesitate to give me a call." He pulled out a business card and tucked it into Chad's thong.

He started to drive off, but then he swung back around.

"Sorry," he said. "Almost forgot to give you this." He handed him the second cucumber back. "Word to the wise: don't forget the lube. That cucumber is no joke." He gave him a wink and sped off.

We all somehow kept straight faces until the cop turned the corner.

"Dude!" whispered scooter. "You're a fucking legend!"

He really was. I thought for sure I was gonna have to show that cop my tits to get him to go away. But Chad had handled it like a total boss. And I was getting serious vibes that the cop wouldn't have liked my tits anyway.

"Hell yeah!" Chad adjusted his grip on both cucumbers and put one leg up on the trashcan in front of the sorority. I posed next to him, pretending to suck on the giant dildo, and the rest of the guys got in the picture too.

Slavanka lifted the camera. "Say gulag!" She snapped a photo.

"Alright," I said. "Onto location number 2!"

"Wait," said Chad. "Shouldn't we kill two birds with one stone and get a picture of a topless girl while we're at the sorority?" He looked up at the building.

"I mean…we can kinda do that anywhere. But if you insist." I tossed the dildo aside and pulled the top of my dress down.

Scooter gasped and pretended not to stare.

Watermelon moved his watermelon lower to cover his junk.

And Shakespeare said, "Those are such stuff as dreams are made on, and our little life is rounded with a sleep."

"Was that about my tits?" I asked.

"Huh? Tits?" said Chad. He'd been staring up at the sorority this whole time for some reason. "Whoa!" he yelled when he finally looked back at me. He dropped the cucumbers and grabbed my tits.

"Babe!" I yelled. "You can't go groping me in front of all your friends! That's completely inappropriate."

"I wasn't groping you. I was covering you!"

I laughed. "Mhm. Sure you were." I pulled his hands off of me and posed for the camera.

A group of guys passing by whistled at me and I gave them a little wave.

"Don't make me beat your asses!" yelled Chad. But his lacy red thong made the threat significantly less intimidating. Either way, his jealousy was really turning me on. I loved when he got all territorial.

"Say borscht!" Slavanka snapped the picture and I pulled my dress back up.

"*Now* can we go to location #2?" I asked.

"Yeah."

We piled back into the limo. Tracking Ash down required a slight detour, but it didn't take long to find her trying to blend into a brick wall that was roughly the color of her hair.

Then we were on to the museum.

"Let me off at the front and then circle around to the back door," I said to Ghostie. "Then wait for my signal."

"Nope." Ash shook her head. "No way. I know the start of a heist when I see one. We've already narrowly avoided prison once tonight. I don't want to push my luck."

"I'm not stealing anything. I promise." I hopped out of the limo and ran up to the front door of the museum. It had been closed since 5 pm. But there was still a security guard on duty.

I tapped on the glass to get his attention.

He was too lost in his crossword puzzle to even hear me.

I tapped louder and he looked up. As soon as he saw me, he dropped everything and ran over. He cracked the door and poked his head out.

"How can I help you?"

"I'm on a scavenger hunt. I just need to pop in real quick to take a few pictures. You can watch me the whole time."

He paused. I could tell he was conflicted. "I wish I could help. But if anyone saw it on the security cameras, I'd lose my job."

"I swear it's only like two things. Here, look at the list." I handed the list to him. "The circled items are the ones I wanna do here."

He looked down the list at the circled items: the samurai helmet and posing in the display window.

"Sorry, I can't…"

"Oh yeah," I said. "I'm also gonna fulfill #8 while posing with the samurai helmet. Two for the price of one."

He looked back at the list. And that was when he realized that I'd just told him I was gonna get topless with the samurai helmet. "Alright," he said. "You have five minutes. And I get to be with you the whole time."

"Thank you so much!" I got on my tiptoes and gave him a kiss on the cheek. And then I ran past him to the back door and waved in the rest of my team. We all posed in the window of the gift shop. And then the guard took us to the samurai helmet. I picked it up and put it on.

"Hey," said the security guard. "I didn't say you could touch it."

"Sure you did." I smiled at him and pulled my tits out.

Now it was Chad's turn to be pissed.

"Babe, what the hell? We already did the topless photo!"

"Only because you insisted on showing me off to everyone on that sidewalk, you naughty boy. Speaking of naughty boys…the security guard only agreed to let us in because he knew I'd be getting topless with the samurai helmet." I turned to him and stuck my tits out. "Worth it?"

The guard nodded.

I grabbed a samurai sword off the wall and posed for the picture.

And then we rushed out and got into the limo.

Chad took the list and scanned down it. Then he checked his watch. "Well damn. We're only one hour in and we're almost halfway done."

"Told you I had a plan," I said.

"Actually, we might be more than halfway done." He pointed to #10: Something heinous. "Do you think wearing that priceless samurai helmet counts as something heinous?"

Maybe. But I didn't want it to. "No way."

"Really? I think it might."

"You wearing that thong is heinous," whispered Scooter.

Chad punched his arm. "Don't be jealous that I have the physique to pull it off. Seriously though, the samurai helmet might count."

"It's borderline," I said. "Especially since it overlaps with another list item. Do you really want to risk it?" I certainly didn't want to. Because the heinous act I had planned was going to be the highlight of my night. "By the way, do you remember the number that Adonis wrote on the ball?"

"Why?" he asked.

"Because he needs to come give me a piggyback ride." *And for the heinous act.* I pressed my legs together just thinking about it.

It was going to be absolutely heinous. And oh so fun.

Chapter 8

A HEINOUS ACT
Saturday, Sept 14, 2013

"So do you remember Adonis' number or not?" I asked.

"Nope," said Chad. "But luckily I already have it in my phone. We text every now and then. We're tight like that."

Really? At the football game Chad had made it seem like he and Adonis had talked a few times, but I thought he'd been joking. It seemed much more likely that Chad had immediately put the number into his phone because he desperately wanted to be friends with the most popular guy on campus and then proceeded to text him too many times. But I was curious to see how this all played out.

"Good," I said. "Give him a call and tell him to meet us outside the library."

"Sure thing." Chad hit call. There was no answer, but Chad left a message: "Hey man, Chad here. From the dining hall. And the football game. Anyway, me and my boys have a wild night planned to celebrate your big win today. We'll be at Harvard Yard soon if you wanna come chill." He ended the call. "That should do it."

"Oh, definitely," I said.

"There's no way," whispered Scooter. "Ten thousand dollars says Adonis doesn't show."

"I'll take that bet."

"Hmm…okay. But there's something I want more than ten grand from you." He glanced at Ash.

"You wanna fuck Ash? Deal." We shook on it.

Ash let out a little gasp. She looked absolutely horrified.

"Trust me," I mouthed to her.

"NO!" she mouthed back.

I slid her my phone with the screen open to the text that I'd just sent to Adonis: "I'd love to thank you properly for giving me the game ball today. Meet me and my girls outside the library in ten minutes." There were a few kiss emojis at the end, but what would really seal the deal was the super cute selfie of me from the football game that I'd attached.

"You better be right," said Ash.

"Of course I'm right. There's no way Adonis won't drop everything to hang out with his boy Chad."

Chad gave me a big smile. "Thanks, babe. At least someone here believes in me."

The limo rolled to a stop outside the library, and just like I'd requested, Teddybear was waiting for us in Chad's Porsche that he'd driven back from Newark. It was a sports car, and it was worth more than $100K, so we all stood in front of it for a picture.

"Five pictures down, five to go," I said. The only pictures we still needed were of us dancing in the library, one of us getting a piggyback ride from the captain of the football team, the John Harvard statue, something heinous, and a gryphon statue. The library and John Harvard were right here, there were plenty of gryphon statues back at the club, and Adonis showing up would take care of the other two. We were definitely gonna win. "To the library!" I yelled and we all took off.

I had a hunch that the librarian at the front desk wouldn't appreciate Chad's thong, so while most of the team went to scout out a good spot for the dance party, Teddybear and I went to let Chad in a side door.

"How was the drive?" I asked.

"Fine," replied Teddybear as we turned down a hallway.

"Anything exciting happen?"

"Nope."

"So you didn't get waylaid by any ruffians on the highway? Or encounter any bears?" I didn't know what kind of things happened while driving on a highway, but I assumed it was wild and dangerous.

"No."

"You're acting weird. Which makes me think you're lying. Oh! I know what happened. You got pulled over and had to give the officer a blowjob, didn't you? Speaking of which…Chad almost got arrested for prancing around in his little thong. It was amazing."

Teddybear pinched the bridge of his nose. "I didn't blow any officers."

"Lame." We turned down another hall and arrived at the emergency exit. "Ah, finally! Chad should be right out there." I went to open the door, but Teddybear put his massive hand out to keep it shut.

"Something actually did happen."

"I knew it! Tell me everything."

"So I *did* get pulled over."

"I knew you blew a cop!"

"No. He let me off with a warning. No blowjobs were involved. But when I went into the glove compartment to grab the registration, I found some documents." He paused. "Case law related to invalidating prenuptial agreements."

"Chad's parents are getting divorced?"

Teddybear shook his head. "That wasn't all. There were also a few collection notices. So I made a few calls, and it seems like the Chadwicks are flirting with bankruptcy. Chastity, I'm so sorry, but I think that Chad's proposal to you is part of a scheme to steal your money."

I laughed. "Aw. Teddybear! That's so cute that you're trying to break me and Chad up. But I promise there's nothing to worry about. Chad didn't propose to me. It was just a promise ring." I went to open the door, but he stopped me again.

"Are you sure? Chastity, I'm worried…"

"Teddybear, there's no need to worry about me. I have everything under control."

"But I really think…"

"And even if everything you said was accurate, it wouldn't matter. Because after we win this scavenger hunt, Chad is gonna get into the Gryphon Club. And the Gryphon Club wouldn't dare let one of its members go bankrupt. It would be a black stain on their reputation."

He just stared at me, still blocking my path from opening the door.

Oh, I knew what was going on. He'd been away from me all day. And he just wanted some attention. Traveling all day on the open road with vagabonds must have been a little straining. I stood up on my tiptoes and kissed him.

His arms instinctively wrapped around my waist, pulling me closer. Teddybear was so territorially sometimes. It was one of the many qualities of his that I appreciated. But I didn't have time to spare right now. He could have his way with me once we were back home. I gave him one last kiss and pulled back. "Everything is fine."

"I hope you're right."

"I am. Now let's let Chad in and go have a dance party in the library!"

***

The dance party was extremely lame. We couldn't get far enough away from a librarian to actually play music, so we all just pretended to dance.

But I didn't really care. I was just daydreaming of Adonis the entire time anyway.

"It's the moment of truth," whispered Scooter as we neared the exit. "If Adonis isn't waiting outside…" He stared at Ash.

"He'll be there," she said. But her voice did not sound confident.

He smiled. "I see what's going on here. You just wanted an excuse to climb this beef tower. So you made a dumb bet."

"That is definitely not what is happening," I said. "You really should have more faith in Chad. I mean…would I really date someone lame?"

"I'm still trying to figure that out. There's no way that Adonis is showing up, though. He was definitely trying to give that football to you. I doubt he even knows who Chad is."

"We'll see about that. Ash, will you be taking your winnings via PayPal or do you prefer cash?"

"Cash will do," she said.

Scooter laughed. And then his jaw dropped. Because Adonis was standing outside the library.

I knew he was huge, but he looked even bigger now that he wasn't down on a football field surrounded by other players. And he was rocking the hell out of those jeans.

I ran over to him. "Fancy meeting you here."

He smiled down at me. "I was surprised to hear from you. When that random asshole snatched the ball from you I thought I'd missed my chance."

"Your chance at what?"

His eyes scanned my body. "Getting to know you."

"Mhm. Sure."

"Hey man," said Chad. "Thanks for coming."

Adonis looked deeply confused as Chad pulled him in for a bro hug.

"These chumps didn't believe we were friends. Can you believe that?"

"Who are you again?" asked Adonis.

"Chad. You know. From the dining hall. We were joking about how chickpeas look like squirrel testicles. Oh, right. You probably don't recognize me in this." Chad pointed to his thong and laughed. "It's a final club thing."

Shakespeare flipped through his book. "Is this a dagger which I see before you, the handle toward your hand?"

"Is that your way of saying that Adonis definitely has no idea who Chad is?" whispered Scooter.

"Of course he knows who I am," said Chad.

"What do you guys think," asked Scooter. "Should Chad be addressing Adonis as a person of authority?"

Everyone on our team nodded.

"Alright, Daddy," said Chad. "How about you give me a piggyback ride over to the John Harvard statue to show everyone how good friends we are."

Adonis shook his head. "Yeah, I'm definitely not gonna do that. And did you just call me Daddy?"

"I'll take a piggyback ride," I said.

"Sure." He bent down to let me climb on. And I savored every second of it. I let my hands explore his back muscles before hopping up and clasping my arms over his rock hard chest.

He effortlessly stood back up and started running.

"Hey!" yelled Chad. "Come back!" But he couldn't keep up with Adonis. It only took like one block to lose him.

"Is he gone?" asked Adonis.

"Yup," I said.

He slowed to a walk. "Oh thank God. Do you have any idea what the hell just happened back there?" he asked.

"We're doing a scavenger hunt for the Gryphon Club."

Adonis laughed. "You're pledging the Gryphon Club? Since when do they accept girls?"

"They don't accept normal girls. But I'm not normal."

"I can see that. You know that the task of getting a piggyback ride from the captain of the football team is usually accomplished by climbing the statues by the stadium, right?"

"Yeah, but I'd much rather climb you. And where are you going? The John Harvard statue is that way." I pulled on his ear to get him to turn left.

"Did you just pull on my ear to try to make me turn?"

"Yup. Would you have rather me used my tongue?" I leaned over and swirled my tongue around the edge of his ear. Then I nipped at his earlobe.

He shivered a little. "Yeah, I definitely prefer that." He made a hard left. Like...*too* hard of a left. So I had no choice but to nip at his right ear too to get him back on course.

The cheeky bastard kept making wrong turns so I'd have to keep licking his ears, but eventually we made it to the statue.

The rest of the group was already there waiting for us.

We posed for a picture with me still on his back and then I hopped off.

"Alright," I said. "Only two pictures left."

"Actually three," corrected Chad. "A gryphon statue, the statue of John Harvard, and something heinous."

"Any ideas for what heinous thing we should do?" asked Watermelon.

"Yeah," whispered Scooter. "Let's go eat a pizza on a treadmill. Or lift some free weights and not wipe our sweat off when we're done." He shuddered at the thought.

"That's one idea," I said. "But why waste time going to the gym when we can do something heinous right here?"

"You want to deface the John Harvard statue?" asked Chad.

"Ten grand says I can rip his head off with my bare hands," whispered Scooter.

"We're not destroying any statues, you Neanderthals." *And does Scooter have a gambling problem?*

"Then what did you have in mind?" asked Chad.

I applied some bright red lipstick and smacked my lips together. "I'm gonna blow Adonis."

"Tonight just keeps getting better and better," said Adonis.

Chad blinked and shook his head. "I'm sorry. It sounded like you said you were gonna blow Adonis."

"Damn," said Watermelon. "Cheating on your boyfriend right in front of his face? That really is heinous."

"I would never do that," I said.

"But you just said that you were gonna blow Adonis."

"Right. But Chad is right here watching, so it's not cheating. God, that really would be heinous if I didn't let him watch the show."

Watermelon raised an eyebrow. "If it's not cheating, then what's heinous about it? I guess it is pretty disrespectful to do it in front of the John Harvard statue."

I stared at him. This Watermelon guy was totally nuts. "There's nothing disrespectful about blowing someone in front of a statue. In fact, when they make statues of me someday, I'll feel quite disrespected if no one gets any blowjobs in front of it."

"Very funny," said Chad. "Seriously though, what heinous act do you have planned?"

"I already told you. I'm gonna blow Adonis. But the trick is that it's gonna be a two-part photo. The first will be me blowing him in front of the statue, and the second will be me walking away before he cums." I cringed saying it. It was a clear violation of Rule #24: No blue balls allowed. Finish what you start. But the scavenger hunt called for something heinous, and I wasn't about to let Chad down. So I had no choice but to do it.

"I'm not a huge fan of that last part," Adonis said. "You gotta finish what you start."

Did he know the Single Girl Rules?

Chad glared at me. "No freaking way."

"Why do you seem so upset, babe?"

"Uh…because you just said you want to blow Adonis."

"You think I want to get on my knees and let some guy I barely know jam his huge cock down my throat?"

Adonis smiled.

"Who said he has a huge cock?" Chad asked.

"Look at how tall he is. And how big his feet are. His cock is probably like a foot long." *God, I hope I'm right.* "Sucking on it won't be easy, but I'll do it for you, babe."

Chad shook his head. "No fucking way."

"I'm so confused. Do you not think it's heinous enough? I mean…I *guess* I could let him cum all over me. Ruining this dress would be pretty heinous."

"Nope."

"You're right. Cumstains come out, so they might not count it. Maybe he should just bend me over the statue and tear my dress off while fucking the hell out of me."

"I'm up for any of that," said Adonis.

"Yeah," agreed Watermelon. "That all sounds pretty heinous. Hurry up and choose one, man. We're wasting valuable time." He tapped on his watch and nearly dropped his watermelon.

"Jesus," said Chad. "I'm not gonna let Adonis fuck my girlfriend."

"So the cumshot then?" I asked. *Yes!* This night was shaping up even better than I'd expected.

"No!"

"Well do you have a better idea?" I asked.

"Yes."

We all stared at him.

"We could uh… Um… Oh! You could blue ball me instead."

"I would, but you have to be wearing that thong."

"Someone else could wear it."

"Nope," said all the other guys.

"Just let her blow Adonis," whispered Scooter.

"Uneasy lies the head that sucks the dick," added Shakespeare.

"See?" I said. "Shakespeare gets it. I'm the one doing all the hard work here."

"What if she just kisses him?" suggested Ash.

"Sweet, innocent Ash," I said with a shake of my head. "A kiss would hardly be heinous."

"I don't love it," said Chad. "But a kiss could actually work. As long as it looks like you're doing it behind my back."

But I want to blow him! I restrained myself from stomping my foot. And a kiss really did not seem heinous. Although Chad hadn't specified *where* I was supposed to kiss him… "Alright," I said. "I'll kiss Adonis on the statue while you guys pose in front of it."

Adonis gave me a lift onto the base of the statue and then hoisted himself up. The rest of the group crowded around the base.

Chad glared back at us.

"Hey!" I said. "No peaking. It's only heinous if it's behind your back."

He turned to face the camera.

"Ready?" asked Slavanka.

"One sec," I called. Adonis leaned down to kiss me, but I put my hand out to stop him. I unzipped his jeans with my other hand. He looked so freaking excited as I dropped to my knees and yanked his pants down.

Holy. Shit.

I couldn't help the smile that spread across my face at the sight of his massive cock. My guess about it being a foot long hadn't been far off.

"What's taking so long back there?" asked Chad.

"Sorry, babe," I said as I slid my hand along Adonis' thick shaft. "Just making sure our pose is perfect." I winked up at Adonis. "I don't want to have to kiss him twice." I pushed on Adonis' hips to turn him a little and then wrapped my lips around his tip. It was so hard not to jam it all the way down my throat, but then the picture wouldn't capture his beautiful length.

I gave Slavanka a thumbs up.

"Say Kremlin!" she said and snapped the picture.

"Thank God it's over," said Chad. He started to turn around.

"Wait!" yelled Slavanka. "Picture blurry. Need another."

God I loved that bitch. I held my pose while she snapped another.

"Still blurry," said Slavanka. She winked at me. We both knew the pictures were fine. She was just giving me more time to have some fun with Adonis. I leaned forward and let his cock slide down my throat. Inch by inch. I locked eyes with him and swirled my tongue around.

He looked like he was in heaven. He buried his fingers in my hair as he stifled a groan.

Told you I was good with my tongue.

I pulled back and then jammed it down my throat again. My gag reflex had been gone for years, but I knew that guys liked it. So I gagged a little.

"What was that?" asked Chad.

"Say AK-47!" yelled Slavanka and snapped another photo. Which gave me just enough time to stand up.

Adonis got his pants up *just* as Chad turned around.

"Hey babe," I said with a saucy little smile.

"Were you just gagging?"

"Yup. Right before that last photo Adonis tried to slip me some tongue." I slapped him.

"Dude, what the hell?" said Chad.

Adonis laughed and rubbed his hand along his cheek. "Sorry. She's just so hot." He winked at me.

"Damn right she is. But she's all mine."

"You're right. That's my bad."

Chad turned back around.

Adonis looked at me and raised an eyebrow.

"What's that look for?"

"You're wild."

"That wasn't wild. That was just me being a good girlfriend and helping my man get into the Gryphon Club."

"Mhm."

"If you wanna see wild, just wait until I sneak into the locker room after your next victory." I leaned forward so I could whisper in his ear. "I can't wait to feel you inside of me." I gave him a kiss on the cheek where I'd slapped him and went to hop off the statue.

But he grabbed my waist to stop me. "I should probably warn you about something…"

"I know your teammates will be there. That's part of the fun."

His eyes lit up. But then he shook his head. "It's not about that. It's about the Gryphon Club. The thong and cucumber thing is a test. If anyone gets stuck with that stuff in a majority of the pictures, the Gryphon Club automatically eliminates them. They want bosses in their ranks, not bitches."

"Well that's not ideal. Chad wore that thong in every single picture. Anything else I should know?"

"I'm 99% sure he's screwed. But they won't formally eliminate him until after the victory dinner. He has until then to charm the punch masters."

"Got it. Do they like jokes? Name dropping? Heckling the help?"

"Definitely not the last one. The punch masters *are* the help. Or at least, they'll pretend to be. They always dress up as the waiters so that they can see how prospective pledges treat the help."

"Oh. In that case, this'll be easy."

"It will?"

I nodded.

"How?" And then his eyes went to my body. "Oh. You're gonna fuck them, aren't you?"

I put my hand to my chest. "Adonis, please. I'm a proper lady. I wouldn't just fuck some random waiter. But I do love sucking cock."

He laughed. "Damn it. I wish I'd volunteered to be a punch master this year."

"Me too. Byeeee." I blew him a kiss and jumped off the statue. "To the Gryphon Club!" I yelled to my team.

Chapter 9

YUMMY WAITER MAN
Saturday, Sept 14, 2013

Chad tapped the eagle head knocker against the massive wooden door of the Gryphon Club. We'd snapped a picture with a gryphon statue in record time. There was no cock sucking or anything fun though. #Lame.

The little window slid open and two eyes peered out at us. "Back so soon?"

"We're done," said Chad.

"As in...you quit?"

"No. We have all ten photos."

Another little window slid open on the door and a hand popped out. "Camera, please."

Slavanka put the camera in the hand.

"Wait here." Both windows slid shut.

Chad backed away from the door and put his arm around me. He'd been acting super possessive ever since we left the John Harvard statue. The thought of me kissing another guy made him go all cave man, and I was loving it.

I couldn't even imagine what would have happened if he'd turned around and seen me with Adonis' huge cock in my mouth. He probably would have punched him. If he kept acting so manly, maybe I'd actually consider marrying him.

Truth be told, I'd already been playing around with wedding invitations. Kind of. The graphics were still wedding-y, but I'd adjusted the text to be an invitation of a different sort. They were *SO* cute. I definitely should have given one to Adonis, but I'd been too distracted by his huge cock in my mouth.

I'd have to mail him one.

I was about to make myself a reminder on my backup phone when the door swung open and a hooded figure walked out.

"Come with me," he said. He spun on his heel and disappeared into the mansion. We all followed him to a formal dining room. The table was so long that it must have been inspired by Adonis' cock. Seriously, three chandeliers fit easily over it. They probably could have fit five.

A dozen hooded figures and their dates for the evening - probably the girlfriends of the other pledges - were seated on one side of the table. The other side was empty.

The hooded man at the head of the table stood up. "Welcome back," he said. "Please, take a seat." He motioned to the empty side of the table.

I took a seat between Chad and Ash. Chad immediately slid his hand onto my thigh.

So possessive.

"I'm pleased to inform you that you are the first team back," continued the man. "And more importantly, we've reviewed your images and determined that you fulfilled all the criteria. Congratulations on not being completely inept." He shook his head. "Actually, I take that back. Usually it's fun being a hard ass and making fun of our pledges, but there's no getting around this. You guys kicked ass tonight. No team has ever completed the hunt in less than four hours. And you guys did it in less than two. Bravo." He raised his drink.

"All because of you," whispered Chad.

Damn right.

"What was that?" asked the hooded man.

Chad stood up. "I was just congratulating my teammate, Daddy. She was the one who figured out the optimal path."

"She's your girlfriend, yes?"

"She is."

"Then based on a few of those pictures, I'd say you're either very brave or very stupid."

"He's brave," I said. "I may have plotted the course, but we all would have ended up in jail if Chad hadn't looked a cop dead in the eye and called him Daddy."

Some of the hoods laughed. But I was more focused on the reaction of the five waiters standing around the table with their hands clasped behind their backs. According to Adonis, they were the real decision makers tonight. And none of them had laughed.

"I'm excited to hear more about that," said the guy at the head of the table. "But first let's place our dinner orders."

I looked down at the menu. It all sounded great, so I spent more time checking out the waiters. They were all handsome in a preppy Harvard guy kinda way. But one stood out above the rest. And by that I mean he had a great bulge in his pants.

I put my hand up to call him over.

"Ready to order, miss?" he asked.

"I am. I'll have the crab cakes." What I really wanted was to lick his cologne off him, but I couldn't exactly order that. Seriously, what was that smell? It was like a mix between pineapple and coconut.

"May I interest you in a beverage this evening? Our house special is the Flying Gryphon."

"Do you have anything with coconut?" I asked. His scent had taken over my brain.

"Technically no." He lowered his voice to a whisper. "But I'm sure I could slip behind the bar and whip you up my signature cocktail. It's like a piña colada, but with a twist."

"That sounds amazing." Mainly because I had a feeling it was going to taste exactly like he smelled.

"I'll have the same," said Ash. "But a virgin one."

"Excellent choice, ladies." He took our menus. "And you, sir?"

"Still looking," said Chad without looking up. He waved him off.

Damn it, Chad! Be nice!

I laughed. "Please excuse my boyfriend. The better the options look, the more he forgets his manners. If anything, you should take his rudeness as a compliment."

"Of course." The waiter bowed slightly and backed away from us. His cologne lingered, but not nearly long enough.

I shoved Chad's leg. "You should really be nicer to the waiters," I said.

"Yes, yes," agreed Slavanka. "Be nice to yummy waiter man."

"He seemed average," said Chad. "And I might have been nice if he hadn't started flirting with you right in front of me."

"Babe, he wasn't flirting with me."

"Oh really? Then what do you call that bullshit about making a piña colada just for you?"

Flirting. He'd 100% been flirting with me. But I couldn't admit it to Chad when he was in his sexy jealous caveman mood. "He was just doing his job."

"Well, he better do his job in a less flirty way or he's gonna get punched in the face."

"Who's gonna get punched?" asked one of the hooded guys.

Chad looked back. "That waiter. He was just hitting on my girl."

"I punched a waiter once," said the guy. From there, the conversation devolved into Chad and a few of the hoods trading stories about ways that they'd abused their employees.

Teddybear and Ghostie are so lucky that I treat them so nice. Sure, I was hard on them. But I also let them be hard on me, if you know what I mean.

Anyway, it seemed like the conversation was going well. In fact, Chad was having so much fun with his new friends that he didn't even pay attention when the waiter came back with our drinks. I ordered him the steak and a scotch on the rocks.

"Oh my God," said Ash. "These piña coladas are amazing."

I took a big sip from my martini glass. It was an odd choice of glass for a piña colada, but I didn't care. Because Ash was right. "They really are delicious."

"What do you think his secret ingredient is?" I asked.

She took another sip. "I think I'm getting a hint of banana."

Banana juice? If it was, then there about a 100% chance that Ash would end up face down on the table getting railed by every member of the Gryphon Club.

But she had requested a *virgin* piña colada, which meant that hers couldn't have any banana juice in it.

We were almost done with our drinks when the waiter came back.

"Told you it was good," he said. "May I get you ladies a refill?"

"As long as you're not planning on taking this one from me, then yes, I'd like another."

"I wouldn't dare take a beautiful woman's drink."

Chad looked over and scowled at him. "I need a refill too."

The waiter looked confused. All of Chad's glasses were full. "Of which beverage, sir?"

"My scotch."

"But your scotch is full, sir."

"Is it?" asked Chad. "I don't think it is." He took his drink and tossed it right in the waiter's face. "Now quit flirting with my girl and bring me another."

"Ah!" I screamed as some scotch splashed onto my dress. I pushed back from the table and shook my arm off.

To his credit, the waiter didn't flinch. "Of course, sir," he said. "I'll have another scotch for you right away." He bowed and left the dining room.

"I'm gonna go clean up," I said. I grabbed what was left of my drink and headed for the bathroom.

"Shouldn't you go help her?" asked one of the other girls at the table.

I didn't catch his answer, but apparently it was no. Because Ash was the only person to follow me.

"Are you okay?" she asked.

"Girl, I'm better than fine. I love when Chad gets all territorial."

"Hmmm…I guess I wouldn't hate having a guy get all pissed at a waiter for flirting with me."

"Right? Although I'm pretty sure he just made his path into the Gryphon Club a lot more difficult."

"Oh?" asked Ash as we pushed into the ladies room. "It seemed like the guys thought it was funny."

"I'm pretty sure they were laughing at Chad rather than the waiter. Adonis told me that the waiters are actually the punch masters. And this is a test to see how the pledges treat them."

"Oh shit."

"Yeah. Oh shit is right." I went over to one of the sinks and started dabbing at the spot on my dress. "There is a silver lining, though."

"How?"

"Well, first of all, can I just say how proud I am of you for following Single Girl Rule #3 to a tee? You were on top of that."

Ash smiled. "Yeah I was!"

I gave her a high five.

"But also…maybe the test isn't as simple as being nice to the waiters. Me blowing Adonis in that picture and Chad wearing a thong the entire time had them wondering if he was brave or stupid. What if the waiter was flirting with me on purpose to see if Chad would stand up for himself?"

"I think it's more likely that he was flirting with you because you look amazing in that dress."

"How amazing?" I asked.

"I don't know. Amazing. Ten out of ten."

I stared at her.

She stared back. And then she laughed. "Oh right. Here." She reached out and honked my boobs.

"Girl, I'm so proud of you," I said. "You just used two different single girl rules in the span of like two minutes."

"I did, didn't it?" Ash looked so proud of herself.

"Wanna go three for three and help me ensure that Chad gets into the Gryphon Club?"

"That depends heavily on the rule you're hoping to invoke."

"Rule #25: Don't be ashamed to use sex to get what you want."

"That's gonna be a hard pass for me."

"Are you sure? Wait! You'd really be going four for four. Because if you help me out here, we'd also use Rule #28: All girls should try at least one threesome. I know you seemed keen on that earlier when we were at the football game."

"Did you hear that?" asked Ash. "It sounded like someone walking with a tray of food. Which means it's crab cake time!"

A likely story. "Okay, you can go eat your crab cakes. But I have one request."

She laughed and honked my boobs again.

"Aw, thanks. But I didn't need another compliment. What I really need is for that hot waiter to bring me a few more napkins."

"But there are plenty right there."

I grabbed them all and stuffed them in the trash. "Not anymore."

"Oh. Oh! I see what's happening here. I'll send him right in. Good luck!" She walked out of the bathroom.

I slid my dress off and fixed my makeup in the mirror. My sexy waiter who smelled like pina coladas would be arriving any second.

Chapter 10
PIÑA CUMLADA
Saturday, Sept 14, 2013

"Come in!" I called when I heard the knock on the bathroom door. "But don't look."

I checked my naked body in the mirror once more. That red dress had looked amazing on me, but I looked even more amazing in only my heels.

The door swung open and the waiter walked in. He kept one hand over his eyes while he waved the other around to make sure he didn't bust his face on anything.

With each step, the aroma of coconut and pineapple grew stronger.

"Where are you?" he asked, still inching forward and waving his hand around.

Rather than answering, I just stepped into his path. His hand collided with my naked breast.

He squeezed it.

I screamed.

He opened his eyes.

I screamed again and covered myself. "I said not to look!"

"I didn't mean to," he said. "It was just a reflex when I ran into you."

"You're still looking."

He turned away. "I'm so sorry."

"You're still looking at me in the mirror." I gave him a saucy smile in the mirror. "Do you like what you see?"

He nodded.

I let my hands fall to my sides. "How about now?"

"Holy shit."

I leaned against the vanity, arching my back. "Did you bring my napkins?"

"Yeah." He turned to me and pulled a stack of napkins out of his serving apron.

I took them and tossed them onto the counter. "Thanks. But I actually needed something else."

"What can I get for you?"

"Is it too late to change my dinner order?"

He looked confused. "Probably. But I'll make an exception for you. Would you like a rib-eye instead of the crab cakes?"

"No." I arched my back even more. "I want you to lift me onto this counter and eat my pussy."

His eyes traveled down my body. "Of course, miss. But that's more of an appetizer for me than an entrée for you. Would you like to hear our dinner specials?"

"Sure."

"So first we have a lovely crab bisque." He took a step toward me. "And we also just added a footlong wiener."

"I like the sound of that second one."

"I thought you might." He untied his apron and then let his tuxedo pants fall to the floor. His cock was already at full attention. To call it a foot long was a bit of an exaggeration. It was probably just over eight inches. But what really intrigued me was the head to shaft ratio. The head was so thick that it almost looked like the top of a mushroom. I bet it would feel amazing sliding in and out of me.

"Well that looks absolutely delicious. I'll have one of those."

"Excellent choice. Let me just lock the door…"

"Don't," I said.

He looked at me.

"I like getting caught. Now get over here and try your appetizer." I jumped up on the counter and spread my legs for him.

"It would be my pleasure," he said as he got to his knees. And then he started feasting. It was like he'd just eaten his favorite dish and now he was licking the plate clean.

"Oh God," I moaned. "Don't stop."

And he didn't. He just kept going. And going. And going.

He pushed on my thighs, spreading them even farther.

God, I wanted even more. I lifted my legs, wrapping them around the back of his neck. He didn't seem to mind at all.

This was by far the best service I'd ever received at a restaurant. It almost made me feel bad about how all of this was going to end. But not quite. Because as much as I was enjoying this, it wasn't about my pleasure. It was about getting Chad into the Gryphon Club.

"I'm ready for my entrée," I said.

He ignored me. Or maybe he just hadn't heard me because my thighs were pressed so tightly against his ears. I spread my thighs a bit and said it again, but he still kept going until. He looked up at me as he thrust his tongue even deeper inside of me. And I wasn't sure if it was his tongue, the confident way he was staring at me, or the fact that I'd been so fucking horny all night that made me shatter so quickly. Scratch that, it was his tongue. His tongue was pure perfection and I never wanted him to stop.

My thighs slammed together to keep him from escaping. And as an added bonus, his nose rubbing against my clit gave me another orgasm.

He kept licking me until my muscles relaxed again.

And then he stood up.

My chest rose and fell as I tried to catch my breath. I'd desperately needed that after today.

"Your entrée is ready, miss." He stroked his cock and looked at me.

Yes, please. I slid off the counter and dropped to my knees. And then I swirled my tongue around the huge head of his cock. It was so soft compared to his rock-hard shaft. I slid it farther into my mouth and tried to imagine what it would feel like inside of me. My guess was that it would be like a ribbed condom, but like a million times better.

I looked up at him and pushed his cock into one cheek. He tasted exactly like he smelled - like coconuts and pineapple.

"How are you enjoying your dinner, miss?" he asked.

I moaned on his cock and his whole body shook. And then I slid back. "It's so big that I'm having some trouble swallowing. Could you help?" I grabbed his hand and put it on the back of my head.

He gave my head a gentle push onto his cock. But that wasn't what I wanted. I wanted him to fuck my face. So I put my hand on top of his and pushed.

"Oh fuck," he groaned as his cock slammed into the back of my throat. But unlike usual, it didn't feel like getting punched. His huge head acted kind of like a little airbag.

Oh hell yeah. This was gonna be the best blowjob I'd ever given.

I pulled my head back and helped him force me down again. And then he didn't need any more help. His fingers tightened in my hair and he started fucking my face. Faster and faster.

I smiled to myself as he leaned back and groaned with pleasure. If Adonis was telling the truth about this guy being a punch master, then Chad was 100% getting into the Gryphon Club. I just had to execute the rest of my plan…

I reached up and played with his balls as he kept fucking my face. And then they started to tense up. He was about to cum. So I gagged and pulled back.

"Fuck," he said. "Don't stop."

I looked up at him. "Wanna bend me over the sink? Or would you rather cum all over my face?"

He smiled and stroked his cock. "Can I do both?"

"Of course you can." I stood up. "But…not today." God, I couldn't believe I was breaking two rules at once. Giving him blue balls was bad enough. Especially because it was the second time I was breaking Rule #24 again in one day. But I was also breaking Single Girl Rule #27: If he makes you come, he can cum anywhere he wants. It wasn't right. I should be drenched in his cum right now. But I'd make it up to him.

"What?"

"My boyfriend loves the idea of me sneaking off to blow other guys. That was why he spilled the drink on us. To get us alone in here so I could give you a special tip."

"Really?"

Hell no. "Mhm. He's a brave man to let me sneak around like this. But he's not stupid. He wouldn't let some random dude fuck me. But I really love your cock, so I'll let you in on a little secret." I grabbed his cock and leaned in to whisper in his ear. "Sometimes he shares me with his friends."

"So if I want to fuck you, I have to be his friend?"

"Yeah. Or…" I paused and then shook my head. "No, that wouldn't work. You're not part of the Gryphon Club. You're just a waiter."

"What if I was a member?"

"Well…if you and Chad were part of the same brotherhood, then of course he'd let you fuck my brains out." I pulled a gold foil envelope out of my purse and handed it to him. "Here."

"What's this?"

"Open it."

He slid the invitation out of the envelope. "A wedding invitation?"

"Not quite." The design was certainly based on a wedding invitation. But I'd turned it into something so much more fun. I took it from him and read: "You and a guest are cordially invited to fuck Chastity Morgan at a date, time, and location of your choosing."

He raised an eyebrow.

"Of course, there's always some fine print too." I kept reading: "Must be 18+. Not valid for residents of FL, GA, or AK."

The waiter laughed. "What do you have against southerners and Alaskans?"

"Nothing. But Daddy's lawyer advised me that those states have certain laws that might view this invitation as a form of illegal prostitution. Anyway…" I cleared my throat and kept reading. "Voucher has no cash value, but may be transferred or sold. Suggested retail price: $1M per guest. All male guests must have at least 8 abs and 8 inches."

He smiled and unbuttoned his shirt to expose his lovely 8-pack. "Looks like I qualify."

He did indeed. And that was kind of the whole point of the invitation. Single Girl Rule #8 forbid me from refusing any man with 8 abs and 8 inches. So this piece of paper really didn't change anything.

"It says that I can fuck you at a place and time of my choosing. I choose…here. And right now."

"Hmm…there's just one problem." I pointed to the final line of fine print.

He looked back down. "This invitation is only valid once Chad Chadwick is a member of the Gryphon Club."

"Sorry," I said. "But rules are rules."

"Damn it."

"As soon as Chad becomes a member, though…you and a guest are gonna have one hell of a time. Think you can help him get initiated?"

"Maybe." He scanned the invitation again. "But I'm not the only punch master."

"You're a punch master?" I asked, trying to sound surprised. *Thanks for the tip, Adonis.*

He nodded. "I am. And Chad definitely has my vote, but I'll still need to convince the other four. The other waiters."

"Maybe I can help." I fished a pen out of his discarded apron and changed the first line of the invitation. Now instead of one guest, he could bring four. "How's that?" I asked.

His eyes got wide when he saw what I'd changed. "That should definitely help."

"Good. Send me a text when you're ready to RSVP." I pointed to my number under the RSVP section of the invitation. "And try not to take too long. Because I *really* want to fuck you." I handed him the invitation and started putting my dress back on.

"Wait," he said. "What am I supposed to do with this?" He motioned to his erection. The thought of sharing me with the rest of the punch masters must have excited him, because he looked like he was about two seconds away from cumming everywhere.

I wanted nothing more than to push him on the floor and ride his beautiful cock. But then all of my hard work would be wasted. I was *this close* to getting Chad into the Gryphon Club. I couldn't back down now.

Or maybe I could…

Single Girl Rule #24: No blue balls allowed. Finish what you start. I'd already broken that rule once with Adonis. Could I really break it again in good conscience? And in combination with Rule #27?

I looked down at the waiter's cock.

God, I wanted him inside of me so badly. Would it really be so bad to bend over the counter for him? Just for a second? The Single Girl Rules demanded it…

Or not.

Unfortunately for me, Rule #24 didn't specify that the finishing had to be done in a timely manner. And Rule #27 was the same…I just had to let him cum wherever he wanted *eventually*. And now that he was in possession of that invitation, there was no way he wouldn't be fucking me soon.

So I wasn't breaking any rules by not fucking him. Maybe I could still get a little taste of cum, though…

"Sorry," I said. "I can't help you with that. But it would be a shame to waste such a delicious treat. And I do need a refill…" I downed the rest of my piña colada and handed him the glass. "Maybe you can fill this up for me?"

"With…" He gestured to his erection.

"Is that your special ingredient? Yum." I winked at him and walked out of the bathroom.

"What took so long?" asked Chad when I sat back down at the table.

"Sorry. That scotch was a bitch to get out of my dress. And then I stopped by the bar to get a refill."

"Where is it?" he asked.

"The waiter said he'd bring it out in a second. He had to mix up a fresh batch."

"Well I hope he brings me another scotch too. That asshole never brought me my refill."

"I'm sure one of the other waiters will help you if you ask *nicely*." I looked around for one of them, but they were nowhere to be seen.

That's odd. The rest of the night they'd all been standing at attention around the table just waiting to serve us. Maybe things were different now that dinner had been served.

I turned to Ash. "Thanks again for coming to the bathroom with me."

"Did everything work out okay?"

I nodded. "It was more than okay." I held up my hands to show her just how okay it had been. And by that I mean I showed her how big the waiter's dick was.

Her eyes got huge. And then something hit me.

"Oh my God!" I said.

"What?" asked Ash.

I looked over at Chad. He was deep in conversation with some of his new hooded friends. So I could say whatever I wanted to Ash and Slavanka as long as I kept my voice down.

"I think I figured out Rule #3! Slavanka, were there any other translations you could have used instead of 'a friend'?"

Slavanka shrugged. "Yes, yes. Lots of options."

"Is it possible that it could have also been translated as 'your girl'? Because then Rule #3 would have been 'Never let *your girl* go into a bathroom alone.'"

"Is possible, yes."

"I knew it! That changes everything."

"Does it?" asked Ash.

"Yes! Rule #3 is a warning for boys. It makes so much sense. Bathrooms are like...the number one place to fuck a hot stranger. So of course guys should never let their girl go alone."

"I really don't think that's right," said Ash. "It's definitely just normal girl code."

The waiter returning with my drink interrupted our debate. But I was definitely right. I'd finally figured it out!

He placed my martini glass on the table. It had a slightly different hue than my original drink. And I knew that he'd followed my instructions and mixed in my favorite ingredient. Drinking it wasn't as good as letting it explode all over my face though. My skin would have been glowing for weeks.

"Sorry it took so long," he said. "I had to get a few of the other waiters to help me make a fresh batch."

Was he saying that he had the other waiters help him jerk off? Or that they all came in my glass?

I looked at the four other waiters all standing there staring at me. One of them winked at me.

Yeah, they'd definitely all cum in my glass. *Those naughty boys.*

"Why is it so thick?" asked Ash.

"There's *extra* of the special ingredient," I whispered. "#EarnedIt."

"What?"

"It's a cock-tail."

"I know...but...it looks different."

She just wasn't getting it. I leaned in close so we wouldn't be overheard. "All the waiters skeeted in it."

"What?!" she said way too loudly.

I ignored her. "It looks delicious." I took a big gulp of my special piña colada.

Ash made a strangled choking noise.

I had no idea why. Sure, I was a little disappointed that they'd mixed their cum with the actual cocktail instead of giving me a straight cumshot. But the viscosity and saltiness really paired nicely with the sweetness of the coconut and pineapple. I would call this new cocktail a piña cumlada.

Ash started really gagging now. She was probably just jealous. This had to be my new favorite drink. I took another sip. And to give them a little preview of what it would be like to cash in that invitation, I let a little piña cumlada dribble out the side of my mouth and onto my breasts. "Oops," I said, looking down at the spill.

I was about to wipe it up, but Chad grabbed my hand to stop me. "I got it." He leaned down and licked the piña cumlada off of me.

The waiter cringed. A few of the other ones snickered. Ash started dry heaving.

Chad pulled up and made a funny face. "What's in that piña colada?"

"Coconut and pineapple I think."

"And a secret ingredient," added Ash and gagged again. The poor girl looked like she was struggling to breathe so I slapped her on the back. She was definitely just jealous she hadn't gotten any.

"Huh," said Chad. "It's a little salty. But I kinda like it." He reached for my glass, but I snatched it away from him.

"Get your own." I downed it before Chad could embarrass himself anymore. Me drinking a beverage spiked with cum was hot. But Chad doing it? Yeah…no one wanted that.

But you know what I did want? More cum.

And to get fucked.

I looked at the five waiters. What were the odds that they'd make Chad a member tonight so that they could have their way with me? I didn't know exactly what they usually used their sex altar for, but I desperately wanted to find out.

The guy at the head of the table clinked his knife against his glass and stood. "Gentlemen." He turned to me. "And lady. Congratulations again on your victory in tonight's scavenger hunt. I have some good news and some bad news. Which would you like first?"

"Good," I said. My teammates agreed.

"Very well. The good news is that the field of potential new members has narrowed considerably this evening. We've gone from 24 down to 6." He paused. "The bad news...well, that number is about to shrink again. Only 5 of you will be left standing." He sat down and motioned to the waiters. They disappeared for a moment and then returned with carts stacked high with golden dessert cloches. Or at least...most of them were golden. Six of them were black. And those were served to me and my teammates.

Once everyone at the table had one, the waiters stepped back.

The guy at the head of the table stood up again. "Under those cloches, each of you will find one of two things. If you have a slice of triple chocolate cake, then please enjoy. If, however, you have nothing, then please see yourself out. You are unworthy of the Gryphon Club."

All the hooded figures and their dates removed the lids of their golden cloches. And then they stared at us expectantly.

I looked at the six black cloches.

Adonis had told me that they always eliminated the pledge who wore the thong in the most pictures. That meant Chad was on the chopping block tonight. Or at least...he should have been. But luckily for him, I was the best girlfriend in the world.

I didn't know which cloche was gonna be empty, but I knew it wasn't going to be Chad's.

I pulled the lid of mine to reveal a lovely piece of chocolate cake.

Scooter had one too. And Shakespeare. And the guy who hadn't really talked the whole night. I still didn't know what his pledge mission was.

That left Chad and Watermelon. One of them was about to be eliminated.

They looked at each other and then slowly removed their cloches.

Chad let out a sigh of relief. Watermelon, on the other hand, muttered, "Fuck this," smashed his watermelon on the ground, and stomped out of the dining room.

I smiled at the waiter. Saving Chad from elimination was a good first step. Now he just needed to make Chad a member and cash in on that invitation.

Chapter 11

A CLASSIC DOUBLE VIRGIN
Saturday, Sept 14, 2013

I took the final bite of my chocolate cake and sat back.

I assumed that the waiter would come in any minute and announce that Chad had been selected as the next member of the Gryphon Club.

But they just cleared our plates.

And then we went back to Chad's dorm.

And then we went to sleep.

I still had hope, though. They'd probably show up in the middle of the night in masks and pretend to kidnap him.

But then I dosed off. And woke up the next morning. And flew Daddy's fun jet back to Delaware.

I kept checking my phone, but there was no word from the waiter.

What was he waiting for?

Sure, it was traditional for pledges to get initiated at the end of the semester. But I'd made an extremely convincing argument for him to do it sooner.

I mean…how could he resist getting to fuck me?

Apparently he couldn't. Because on Thursday night I finally got a text from an unknown number.

"Tomorrow night. 9 pm. Gryphon Club. There's a section of wall two blocks west of the main entrance. Knock twice and show your tits to the camera."

I smiled to myself.

A secret door? And the password was my boobs? I very much liked where this was headed.

***

The next night at exactly 9 pm, Ghostie dropped me, Ash, and Slavanka off at the stretch of wall described in the text.

"Are you sure this is where we're supposed to be?" asked Ash. "Because this looks like somewhere that you'd dump a body after chopping it up into little bits. And doesn't going to the Gryphon Club on a Friday night violate all sorts of Single Girl Rules about the sanctity of girls' night?"

"I actually don't think it does. I mean, there's Rule #15: No inviting guys to girls' night…unless they're strippers. But technically we didn't invite any guys to this girls' night. They invited us." I walked up to the wall and knocked twice.

A little camera poked out and looked at each of us.

When it landed on me, I opened my trench coat and pulled my bra down to expose my breasts.

A moment later a section of the wall slid sideways to reveal a secret tunnel.

"Okay," said Ash. "I admit. That was pretty freaking cool. It's like we're in an episode of Inspector Gadget! Although I still don't understand why you didn't wear any clothes under your coat. He definitely always wore a full suit…"

"What do you mean? I'm wearing lots of clothes. Too many, if anything."

Ash gave me a weird look. "A bra and that tiny little skirt hardly count as clothes."

"Uh…you're forgetting about these bomb ass gloves." I pulled my arms out of my coat to flaunt my red, fingerless, opera-length gloves. "And this isn't just some ordinary bra.

This is special order from Odegaard, hand crafted with lace styled in the shape of gryphon feathers."

Slavanka honked my boobs.

"Thanks, girl. You too." I honked her back.

Unlike Ash, who was sporting a T-shirt and leggings under her trench coat, Slavanka knew what was up. I was honestly a little jealous that she got to wear a full set of lingerie. But alas…in honor of General Orville Thunderstick III, I wasn't allowed to wear panties. So instead I had to settle for a tiny little schoolgirl skirt.

We walked through the secret passage, our heels clicking and echoing with each step. And by *our* heels, I of course mean mine and Slavanka's. Ash was in sneakers.

Eventually we got to what looked like a reception desk carved into the stone wall. A hooded man was sitting behind it.

"Good evening, ladies. May I take your coats?"

"I'd prefer to keep it on," I said.

"I keep on too," said Slavanka.

"Oh come on, guys," said Ash. "Why are you so afraid to take your coats off? Oh wait, is it because you're dressed super inappropriately underneath? Booyah!" She made a show of untying her trench coat and letting it fall to the floor.

I laughed. "I'm not afraid to take it off. I just had a whole reveal planned. It would be a shame to spoil it just because some pervy coat check wants to get an early peek at the goods."

"Ah, I see," said the guy. He turned around and pulled three hooded capes off a rack. They were similar to the robes that the brothers wore, but the material seemed even richer. And they were capes instead of robes. And they had a super cool claw-shaped clasp.

"Oh hell yeah." I tore off my coat and replaced it with the cape. The material was so freaking soft. Was it velvet?

Once we were all enveloped in our plush capes, the guy pressed a button and another secret door slid open.

I expected another hallway. Or a staircase. Or a dance floor. Instead, we were in a state-of-the-art control room. Three rows of hooded figures all typed away at keyboards, occasionally looking up at the massive wall of monitors.

The one in the middle turned around and cocked his head. "Wow. First they let him in early, and now this? Dude must be a total boss."

Ash and I looked at each other. It seemed like maybe he was talking about Chad? But I didn't quite understand all of it.

"There's a locker room down the hall if you need to change or do your makeup or anything," said the guy. "Make it quick, though, I think they're about to begin. And if the lights turn red, get back here immediately." He spun around and started typing again.

"Wanna check out the locker room?" asked Ash.

"Nah, I'm more interested in what's happening here." I pointed to the monitors. One by one, they were coming online. Each showed a different angle of the same room.

"Oh my God!" said Ash. "That's the creepy sex dungeon we found last weekend!"

I stared at the screens in awe. "It's even better than I imagined." Seriously, it was. The round king-sized bed covered in gold satin sheets...the countless candles casting a sexy glow on the intricately carved pillars...the gryphon-shaped throne for the master of ceremonies. It was the perfect sex dungeon.

Drums started playing and dozens of hooded figures began filing in, each chanting as they walked.

It only took a minute for them to form a circle around the perimeter of the room, but on the first floor and up on the balcony.

The chanting intensified as another hooded man walked in. The biggest screen in the command center changed to focus just on him walking to the throne. When the candlelight caught his robe just so, a red gryphon crest flickered to life.

I can't lie - I was super jealous of his robe.

He took a seat on the throne and the chanting immediately ceased. The camera zoomed in on him. His hood was pulled down tight over his face. And he had a gold mask over his eyes. But I recognized that mouth. It was the same mouth that had absolutely feasted on my pussy last weekend.

The punch master.

"Welcome, brothers," he said. "It is not often that we find a man worthy of joining our ranks. But tonight, I'm pleased to announce, we have done exactly that. All five punch masters are in full agreement. This man belongs in the Gryphon Club. And so, without further ado…let the initiation ceremony begin."

The drums and chanting started again and the main image changed to a closeup of Chad entering the sex dungeon. Unlike the hooded brothers, he was dressed only in a white linen robe, and his face was on full display. He knelt in front of the throne.

"Rise," said the punch master. "Tell me, pledge. Why are you here?"

"I desire to become a brother of the Gryphon Club, Daddy."

"And do you understand the full weight of that request?"

Chad nodded. "I do."

"The oath of brotherhood is a lifelong commitment. You shall treat your brothers as if they are your flesh and blood. And you shall never betray them."

"I understand."

"It is a simple creed, yet there is nothing more powerful than the trust we all share. Cherish it. And cherish this first gift we have for you."

The lights in the control room turned red and the guy in the center spun around. "That's your cue," he said.

"Our cue?" I asked.

"We no bring gifts," said Slavanka.

The guy pointed at us. "*You're* the gifts."

"Oh, I love that! Just to be clear, who are we supposed to be having sex with?"

"The dude in the white robe."

Well that's disappointing. I thought tonight was gonna be my night to have some fun with all five of the punch masters. I could have sex with Chad anytime. Although I guess fucking him in front of an audience would spice things up a bit.

I turned to Ash and Slavanka. "Come on, girls! Let's go give Chad the most epic initiation ever."

Ash's eyes got huge. "I'm not gonna lose my virginity to Chad!"

"Why not?" I said. "I'm going to."

"You're not a virgin."

"Sure I am. I haven't had sex all day. And I've never had sex on a sex altar. I'm a classic double virgin here."

"Uh…I'm pretty sure I heard you banging Teddybear in the shower this morning."

"Was that this morning? Huh. I guess it was."

"And anyway, virginity means you've *never* had sex."

I laughed. "Right. That's what it means in like…middle school. But that's an impossible standard in college, so it makes more sense to do it by the day." And then something hit me. "Wait. Whoa whoa whoa. Are you telling me you're a legit virgin? As in, you've never had sex?"

"Of course," said Ash. "I've never even had a boyfriend."

"Holy shit. Girl…we need to fix this immediately. Come on." I tugged on her arm to try to take her out to the sex altar.

She pulled away and hid behind a chair. "I'm not going out there!"

"Why not?"

"Because! There are like a million people watching! And they're definitely filming it. And do you seriously want your boyfriend to take my virginity?!"

Everyone in the control room was staring at her.

"Sure," I said with a shrug. "He actually has a perfect starter dick. He's on the smaller side so it probably won't even hurt."

"No!" she screamed. "No, no, no!"

"Are you sure? Losing your virginity on a sex altar would be totally epic."

"I really hate to interrupt this," said the guy in charge, "because this is the most entertaining conversation I've ever witnessed. But I really need at least one of you to go out there immediately or I'm gonna be in deep shit."

"Okay, okay. I'm going." I started towards the door. "Oh! Before I go out there, any suggestions on which positions look best in this lightning?"

"You'll look amazing no matter what," he said.

I smiled at him. "Yeah I will. You coming, Slavanka?"

"No, no. Bitch boy not my type."

"Fair enough." I pulled my hood down over my face, wrapped my cloak tight around myself, and walked out into the sex dungeon.

All the brothers turned as soon as they heard the click of my heels.

And then they started chanting.

Show time.

Chapter 12
WOMP WOMP
Friday, Sept 20, 2013

I pulled my cape back *just enough* so that everyone could see my legs as I strode towards Chad.

He looked excited. But also a little terrified.

For a second I thought he might get stage fright. But then I pictured my current outfit and realized that him not getting a boner would be literally impossible once I tore off this cape.

I circled around him, slowly tracing my gloved hands over his chest and his back muscles. Not bad, but nothing compared to Adonis'. Speaking of which...

I looked around to see if Adonis was in the crowd. There were definitely one or two guys that were tall enough to be him. But the dim light combined with the hoods and masks made it impossible for me to be sure.

I did another circle around Chad, and then I started to go in for the kiss. At the last second, I pulled back and pushed on his chest. He stumbled backwards, tripping over a stone step, landing on the big round bed. I stepped up in front of him, pushed my cape to the side, and started grinding on him reverse cowgirl.

He got harder with each pop of my hips.

"Oh God," he moaned.

You like that?

I shifted a little so that even more of my weight was on top of him. And then I started twerking like this was my audition for a rap video.

Actually…if I'd been auditioning for a rap video, I definitely would have just immediately dropped to my knees and started sucking his cock. But this performance required a bit more nuance. I needed to honor the sanctity of this sex altar with a proper lap dance before I got to the good stuff.

I arched my back and really pressed up on him.

Chad groaned again. And then his whole body shook. "Oh fuck," he muttered.

And then I felt a wet spot on his robes.

That little idiot just came in his robes!

I mean, I couldn't really blame him. My lap dances were hot fire. But seriously…in front of all his new brothers? Before I even took off my cape? So embarrassing. I couldn't let them find out.

Which meant I had to get him hard again as quickly as possible. And in the process, I couldn't let them see the cum stain on his white linen robe.

I kept twerking on him. But he just got more and more flaccid with each movement.

I wasn't really surprised. Some guys could cum lots in a short period of time. But Chad? His refractory period was like 48 hours.

Damn it!

I busted out my best moves, but nothing was working.

And then the chant slowly changed from some Latin nonsense to "Fuck her, fuck her." It got louder and louder the more Chad refused to comply.

The punch master motioned to one of the brothers, who immediately stepped forward and yanked on my cloak. And then he stopped. "Hold on," he said. "I think he might have cum in his robes."

The punch master stood up and the chanting stopped. "Stand up, pledge," he demanded.

I moved to the side and Chad got to his feet, holding his hands over his junk.

"Move your hands."

He did. Some of the hooded figures laughed at the sight of the little wet spot on his crotch. The linen did absolutely *nothing* to hide the stain. If anything, it made it more obvious.

"Womp womp" said one of the hoods.

"Really, dude?" said another.

"Can't blame him," added a third. "She's a fucking 10."

Aw, thanks!

The punch master shook his head and scratched at his face. "I hate to say this, but you're all dismissed."

The hoods all filed out of the room, leaving me and Chad alone in the sex dungeon with the punch master.

"So…is my initiation complete?" asked Chad.

"I'm afraid so," said the punch master. "And it did not end successfully."

"Huh? What do you mean?"

"Believe me, I was rooting for you more than anyone. But the rules are very strict. Members fly in from all over the country for initiations. So if a pledge refuses or is unable to complete the initiation ceremony before midnight, then they are unworthy of joining the brotherhood. Period. Full stop. Done."

Oooh! Does that mean James Hunter flew in for this event?

"But I did complete it," said Chad. "Even though it was a bit premature, it should still count, right?"

"I usually wouldn't tell you this. But I feel for you. So I'm gonna let you in on a little secret about the brotherhood." He gestured to me. "This beautiful woman was a gift, yes. But she also served a more sinister purpose. Have you ever seen the movie *The Firm?*"

"Maybe?"

"In it, a young lawyer goes on vacation and is seduced by a beautiful woman. But the twist is that she was hired by his new law firm to get pictures of him being unfaithful, which they could then use as blackmail if he ever stepped out of line."

"Oh right," said Chad. "I remember that. Great movie."

"Indeed. Now, since all of our pledges are college students, we don't get too caught up about the whole unfaithful part. But we do still film the initiation and cut it to make it look like you're part of a sex cult. And once our members graduate and become successful politicians and titans of industry, these tapes are exactly the sort of thing that the media would have an absolute field day with. We're talking front page of every major newspaper. Stocks losing millions. CEOs getting fired. Polling numbers taking a nosedive. That sort of thing. But as long as you stay faithful to the brotherhood, then you never have to worry about the tape leaking."

Damn. That's so smart! Sex tape blackmail was the best type of blackmail. Which was why I'd used it to get Teddybear and Ghostie to fall into line.

"What's the problem then?" asked Chad. "You got a great sex tape of me."

"Sorry, man, but you creaming your robes isn't exactly a sex tape."

"You're right. It wasn't a sex tape. But it was still perfect blackmail. You think I'd want this video ever seeing the light of day? *Hell* no."

"I can't argue with that. But again, rules are rules. And Rule #54a of the Brotherhood handbook is very specific: An initiation video must feature the pledge, sex with his gift, and ejaculation."

I pulled my hood back. "I'm so sorry, babe. I shouldn't have twerked so hard on you."

"Chastity?!" yelled Chad. He jumped and narrowly avoided turning the hundreds of candles on the floor into dominos.

I laughed. "Of course it's me. Wait…who did you think was grinding all up on you like that?"

Chad coughed. "Oh. No. I totally knew it was you. I just got distracted by all this sex tape stuff and assumed you'd left."

I stared at him. "Mhm. Suuuuure you did." I turned to the punch master. I knew he didn't want to have to disqualify Chad, because that meant he'd never get to use that invitation. And that would be devastating for him. So I had all the leverage. "Here's an idea. How about we forget this never happened, regroup tomorrow, and take another shot at it? Next time I'll try to take it easy with the lap dance." Although I couldn't make any promises. My lap dances were amazing whether I tried or not.

The punch master shook his head. "No can do. The rules specify that once the initiation ceremony begins, it must be completed by midnight."

"And what time is it now?"

He motioned to a giant clock built into the back wall of the sex dungeon. "Almost 10."

"Then we still have two hours to find a loophole. Where can I get a copy of this dumb rule book?"

"I have one in my room."

"Then let's go!"

We followed him through the mansion halls up to his room and he tossed me a skinny little book.

"Only 200 pages?" I asked. "This'll be easy."

He tilted his head.

"Don't doubt her," said Chad. "She's a freaking genius."

"I hope you're right."

I bet you do. Because if I found a loophole, Chad would become a member. And then he'd get to cash in that invitation.

I curled up on his bed and cracked the book open.

"Aha!" I yelled thirty minutes later. I was kind of ashamed that it had taken me so long, but I'd found the loophole.

And it was a fun one.

Chapter 13

PASS OR PLAY
Friday, Sept 20, 2013

"What's the loophole?" asked Chad.

"It's funny. I just read every rule in this book. But the whole time the loophole was right in the rule that..." I looked at the punch master. "What's your name again?"

"Jack."

"Nice to meet you, Jack." *Again.* "Anyway, the loophole was right in the rule that Jack quoted to us earlier. Rule #54a: An initiation video must feature the pledge, sex with his gift, and ejaculation."

"And...?" asked Chad.

These boys were so dense. "It never states that the pledge has to be the one having sex with his gift. Or that he has to be the one ejaculating."

"But you're the gift."

"I am."

"But that would mean..." A look of shock spread across his face. "Are you seriously suggesting that I should just sit here while you go fuck some random dude in that weird sex dungeon?"

"Of course not!"

"Thank God." He let out a huge sigh.

"There's no way I'd leave you up here and not let you watch. And anyway, Rule #54a requires that the pledge be in the video."

Chad laughed. "Very funny. Seriously, though. We don't have much time. What's the loophole?"

I stared at him. "That *is* the loophole."

"It's definitely against the spirit of the initiation," said Jack. "But I can't argue with your logic. I'll allow it."

"I bet you will," Chad scoffed. "Let me guess…you'll be happy to step in and be the one to fuck her?"

"Babe, don't be rude. Jack's been doing everything he can to help you get initiated."

"Yeah," agreed Jack, trying his best to hide the excitement in his voice.

"But *of course* Jack isn't going to fuck me. Him doing so might be construed as him taking a bribe, which would be a clear violation of Rule #87b. Or at the very least it would be viewed as a conflict of interest. Either way, it would risk invalidating the whole initiation." Really, Jack would have been the perfect choice. I'd been dreaming of riding his cock ever since our little bathroom encounter. But my leverage over him - the way I'd made this initiation happen so quickly - was that he desperately wanted to fuck me. And right now, he could only do that by making Chad a member and then cashing in on that invitation. So my body was off limits to him. *For now.*

"Nope," said Chad. "There's no way I'd let you fuck some random dude."

"*Let me?* You act like I want to do this. That would be so naughty!" I tried to hide my smile. "But I'm the best girlfriend ever, so I'm willing to do whatever it takes to make your dreams come true. And getting into the Gryphon Club has always been your dream." *And fucking a stranger in front of you has always been a dream of mine.*

Chad shook his head. "Of course I want to be a member. But I'll have another chance to join next year."

"I'm afraid not," said Jack. "Pledges have one shot at initiation. If the ceremony isn't complete by the time the clock strikes midnight, it's over."

"Oh well. It's not worth letting Chastity cheat on me."

"Who said anything about cheating?" I asked. "It's just part of a ceremony."

"It's still cheating."

"Oh really? So when you were getting a lap dance from me a few minutes ago, that was cheating?"

"No. Because it was *you* giving me the lap dance."

"Right. But you didn't know it was me."

"Of course I did."

I stared at him. "Did you though? Because you nearly tripped over a candle and lit the entire sex dungeon on fire when I took my hood off."

"Okay, fine. Maybe I didn't know it was you. But it was just a lap dance. You're talking about having sex with someone."

"I actually might have a solution for that," said Jack.

"Oh?" I asked.

"Yeah. I just need to make a quick call." He pulled out his phone and walked to the corner of his room.

I tried to listen, but I couldn't quite make out what he was saying.

"Okay," he said a minute later. He walked back over to us and put his arm around Chad. "I've got some great news for you, my man. I just talked to the Grand Gryphon, and he's agreed to let us do this without all the spectators. So no one but us will know it happened."

"Uh, cool," said Chad. "Still not happening."

"That's not all. He also said a blowjob can count as sex."

Chad got up and pulled on my arm. "Come on, babe. Let's get out of here."

"But didn't you hear him?" I asked. "I don't even have to fuck anyone." *Darn it.* "I'll just give a quick blowjob and then you'll be a member of the Gryphon Club!"

"I know it's a little weird," said Jack. "But it's not like she's never blown anyone else, right?"

"Of course she hasn't. I was her first."

Huh? Surely he didn't actually believe that. He must have just been trying to show off for Jack.

"And have you ever gotten a blowjob from someone else?" asked Jack.

"Yeah. But that was before we met…"

"Then it's only fair if she evens things up."

Chad balled his fists. "Fuck you."

I stepped between them to try to calm things down. "Babe, this isn't about evening things up. I got us into this mess by twerking too hard on you. And I'll never forgive myself if that's the reason why you don't get into the Gryphon Club." I looked up at him with big sad eyes and grabbed his hands. "Please let me do this for you."

Chad sighed and I felt his hands relax.

"I don't know," he said. "I mean…how would you feel if you had to watch some hot girl give me a blowjob?"

Wasn't he already doing that whenever we weren't to-gether? *Sillykins.* There was no reason to put on a show for me. "To get me into a secret club that I'd been dreaming of joining my entire life? I wouldn't even have to think twice about it. Of course I'd let you." I smiled up at him and batted my lashes.

And I knew I'd won. Not that my victory was ever in question. I *always* won.

"Fine," said Chad.

Yes!

"But I have three conditions."

"Anything."

"First, I want to choose the guy. I don't want this ass-hole bringing in some amateur pornstar with a huge dick or some shit like that."

Ooooh! I love the sound of that. But I was willing to compromise. "I should have a say too. It's my mouth."

"Works for me," agreed Jack. "But you'll have to choose from the guys in the building. There's no time to screw around here. What's your next condition?"

"I refuse to call anyone else Daddy tonight."

"To free you from your pledge requirement is highly irregular. But I guess it would be pretty awkward for you to call a guy Daddy while your girlfriend sucks him off. So I'll allow it."

"And your final condition?" I asked.

"After this is over," said Chad, "I want to have a hall pass."

I thought we already had an unlimited amount of those? "Sure. I mean…I don't *love* the idea of you with another woman. But I refuse to give up on your dreams. So you have yourself a deal. Now can we please get started?" I gestured to the clock. We had a little over an hour until the clock struck midnight.

"Great," said Jack. "Let's go find our lucky guy."

Chad followed Jack out of his room, but I hung back to check my outfit in the mirror. I made sure my boobs looked amazing in my bra, and then I pulled my cloak tight around myself. Chad had cum so quickly that I hadn't gotten to do my big reveal for him. But that was okay, because I'd still get to do it for someone else.

I touched up my crimson lipstick and then headed out into the hall.

The boys had stopped in front of the door next to Jack's. The little whiteboard hanging on the door looked horribly out of place next to the old paintings and golden sconces that lined the hallway.

Please be hot. Please be hot, I thought as Jack knocked.

And my wish was definitely granted. I almost had to cross my legs when the door opened. Because *damn.* He was straight out of a magazine. Seriously. His face was model-perfect. And as my eyes scanned down his shirtless torso, I got even more excited. Rock hard pecs. Eight perfectly sculpted abs. And he was rocking the hell out of a pair of jeans.

"Hey, Jack," he said in the world's deepest voice. "What's up?"

Jack shook hands with him. "I wanted to introduce you to my new friends, Chad and Chastity. Guys, this is Mike."

"Nice to meet you," said Mike. He shook hands with Chad and then turned to me. "Wait a second, I recognize you. You were the gift tonight. And he was the initiate."

"Yup!" I said. "That was us."

"I have to say, that was one hell of a performance. I've seen a lot of initiations, and I've never seen a girl twerk so hard that the pledge jizzed his pants."

"Aw, thanks. But you should have seen what I had planned next."

"I wish I had." The smile he gave me would have made my panties fly off...if I'd been wearing any. But I wasn't. #GeneralThunderstick.

"We need your help," I said.

"We *might* need his help," corrected Chad.

Mike ignored him. "Sure thing. What can I do for you?"

Hot damn. This guy was giving me some serious big dick energy. I couldn't wait to see what he was packing. "Long story short, Chad still needs to complete his initiation. But after his little mishap earlier, he can't perform. So we're looking for a stand-in."

Mike looked confused at first. But that quickly turned into pure excitement. "You mean you need someone to fuck you?"

I nodded and gave him my sauciest smile.

"No," said Chad. "No one's fucking you. It's only a blowjob."

Mike took a deep breath and his abs tensed. God, he was so hot. "Well, either way, I'm happy to help."

"I bet you are," scoffed Chad.

"Let me just change back into my robes…" He walked over to his dresser as he started to strip off his jeans.

"What do you guys think?" asked Jack. "Pass or play?"

Chad glared at Mike. "I don't like this guy's energy. Pass."

I was about to protest, but then Mike turned around in only his briefs. And they showed *everything*. Unfortunately, there wasn't much to show. Which was confusing. Because I'd been expecting his cock to be so big that it was hanging out the bottom of his briefs. And I was never wrong about such things. But the evidence was undeniable. Maybe he was a grower. But I wasn't going to take that risk.

Oh well. On to the next guy.

"What's going on?" asked Mike.

"Chad passed," I said. "So it's a no go. Sorry, dude."

We all left and went to the next door. Jack knocked, but no one answered. And no one answered the next door either.

"Damn," said Jack. "It's slim pickings up here tonight. Everyone must already be down at the initiation after-party." He knocked on another door and received no reply.

"Maybe we should go down to the party to find someone?" I asked.

"Those rooms are forbidden to non-members. So Chad wouldn't be able to come. But if he doesn't mind letting you choose…"

"No way," said Chad. "Let's keep looking up here."

We went to the next door. And the next. But I wasn't really paying attention anymore. I was more focused on the paintings of old members. And looking at the drawings on the white boards on each door. Mostly drawings of dicks. Some more impressive than others.

Wait a second!

I looked back at the door we'd just knocked on. The dick drawn on the whiteboard was absolutely massive. With thick veins that would rub me in all the right places. But what really got my attention was the note written above it. Or, more specifically…who the note was addressed to.

Adonis!

I was devastated that he hadn't answered. But I refused to give up hope. "Damn," I said. "This is taking forever. Maybe we should split up?"

Chad and Jack agreed and we all started knocking on doors.

Which gave me the perfect opportunity to double back to Adonis' room.

I knocked on the door again, just to be sure. And when there was still no answer, I wrote him a little note on his whiteboard: "Hey, I need your help with something in the sex dungeon. Eggplant emoji, lips emoji. -Chastity."

Writing out *emoji* didn't have the same effect as a real emoji. But whatever, he'd get the point.

I went down the hall and knocked on the rest of the doors.

They were all empty. But then I heard voices coming from the last door on the hall.

"Hey guys!" I called. "I think I found someone!"

Chad and Jack rushed over.

"That's the bathroom," said Jack.

"Then I guess there's no need to knock." I pushed the door open and walked in. Ash had mentioned that the bathrooms in this place were like the world's fanciest locker rooms, and she wasn't wrong. Well, she was a little wrong. The locker rooms at Daddy's country club were fancier than this. But not by much. So I'd give Ash a pass on this one.

In addition to being fancy, it was also huge. And all the lockers made the place like a maze. I took off down one row while Chad and Jack went to the sinks and stalls.

I didn't find any hot boys, but I did come across a few sets of clothes draped on some benches. And then I heard the voices again. I followed the noise, and as I got closer, the air got thick with steam. And then I was at the shower entrance.

I couldn't wait to see who was inside.

Chapter 14

THE WHOLE QUARTET
Friday, Sept 20, 2013

I stepped in. It was a big communal shower with about a dozen showerheads around the perimeter. More importantly, three of those showerheads were occupied by hot naked men. I couldn't decide which one I liked the most. They all had exceptional butts, but one of theirs was a little tanner than the rest. And I had a thing for tan butts with just the right amount of hair. Most importantly, a tan butt meant the man had to have been nude outside on the regular. And I was vibing that confidence.

"Dude," the guy in the middle said as he rubbed a bar of soap all over his muscles. "Can you believe that idiot jizzed in his pants tonight?"

Tan Butt laughed. "Some guys just can't handle perfection. Were we this lame when we went here?"

Went here? If these guys had already graduated, why were they in this shower? Oh wait, Jack had said that members flew in from all over the country for initiation. So that meant these guys were more…experienced. In every way. And I was here for that.

"I honestly don't remember much of it," the guy with the soap said. "We were all pretty high."

The third guy squirted a huge glob of shampoo into his hands and started working it into a rich lather. "Even when

I'm high, I've never jizzed in my pants. He didn't deserve to fuck such a hot girl. But damn…I would have loved for him to last a little longer so we could've seen what was under her cape."

"I know," agreed Tan Butt. "Did you see the legs on her?" He whistled. "I bet her tits are amazing."

"They are," I said.

All three guys spun around with their hands over their junk. But they didn't seem at all embarrassed. The one with the tan butt even gave me a sexy little smirk.

Oh my God. I recognized that smirk. He was James Hunter's younger brother, Rob! And the other two were frequently featured with them in the tabloids. Mason Caldwell was the guy with shampoo in his hair. And the middle guy was his brother, Matthew.

They were basically NYC royalty. Their dads were two of the richest and most powerful men in New York. Other than Daddy, of course. He had more money than both of their families combined.

I was a little disappointed that James wasn't with them, but it was hard to complain too much. Because these three were drool-worthy.

And I wanted to see if I could actually make them drool. They'd asked to see my tits. I could play along. "Wanna see?" I asked and gestured to my tits.

"Holy shit," said Rob as he gave me the up down.

I wanted to scream "play" but Chad wasn't here. Actually, I wanted all three of them to come with me. The Caldwells both had strong, wide shoulders. And the abs on all three of them…yup…eight abs. And I bet there were eight inches behind their hands. I was about to find out.

I started to pull my cloak open, but then I stopped. "I'll show you mine if you show me yours."

Mason was the first to move his hands. But all the shampoo had created a giant ball of suds on his junk. He winked at me.

The other two moved their hands too.

Oh damn.

I'd hit the dick lottery, because both of them were very well endowed. And based on the size of the suds on Mason, I was pretty sure I'd gone 3/3. Adonis level perfection.

And they were about to get even bigger.

I contorted my body into a super sexy model pose and tore off my cape.

"Oh damn," said Matt. He moved his hands to cover his growing erection.

"No, no, no," I said. "Hands by your sides. Unless you want me to put my cloak back on…"

"Dude, show her your dick," hissed Rob. He grabbed some shampoo and continued showering as if this was a normal night at the Gryphon Club.

Matt laughed and moved his hands.

Very nice.

But I was most interested in what was going on with Mason. Because the ball of suds on his junk was quickly turning into a very large rod of suds pointed directly at me.

"You," I said, pointing at him. "Take a step back into the water."

"Don't you dare," said Chad, bursting into the shower. His eyes went to my bra and skirt. "And what the hell are you wearing?"

"Do you like it?" I asked. I stuck my leg out and the slit in my skirt shifted dangerously close to showing *everything*.

"I do," said Mason.

"Shut the hell up," said Chad. He grabbed my cloak off the floor and tried to put it on me, but I spun away.

"Babe! You're gonna get me all wet."

Mason laughed. "I'll happily get you all wet. Speaking of which…do you still want me to take a step back into the water?"

I loved how flirtatious he was. "Yes please."

"No," said Chad. "You stay put."

Mason looked right at Chad and smiled. And then he took one step back.

"No!" yelled Chad.

Rob started doing a drum roll on his thighs.

And Mason took another step back. The water started to wash over him, slowly exposing the base of his cock.

"Stop! Don't you dare take another step!"

"Why do you want him to stop?" asked Rob. "If you want some bubbles, just ask." He casually walked over and booped Chad on the nose with a very soapy hand.

I stifled a laugh as Chad swung at Rob. But Rob was way too quick.

"I think he hates bubbles," said Mason. "I guess I better get these off of me." He took another step back and now the water was fully on him. Within a second his cock was completely exposed. And it was magnificent. I wanted to lick every drop of glistening water off of it.

Chad glared at him.

"Hey dude," said Mason. "Don't be mad at me. She told me to do it. I was just following orders."

"That's true," Matt said. "I think your girl is looking for an upgrade."

"No." Chad turned to me. "Why the hell did you want to see his dick so badly?"

"I didn't. But I figured you would so you can decide which one you want me to suck."

Matt gave me a cocky smile. "Did you just say you're gonna suck one of our dicks?"

"She definitely did," said Rob. His cock stiffened even more.

I swallowed hard, wishing Rob's cock was already down my throat. And Matt's. They were both growing by the second.

"She can suck mine any time," said Mason.

Yes please.

"Honestly," said Chad. "I was going to choose you because you're short and ugly."

Mason wasn't either of those things. He was tall and fit and his face deserved to be carved into a statue and displayed in a museum for all to see.

"But since you were an asshole and stepped back into the water, it's a pass for me."

Damn! I wanted all three of them. I wanted to squeeze Rob's tight little ass. And run my hands down Matt's washboard abs. And see Mason's face when I pressed his cock into the back of my throat. But Chad had just passed on Mason. How could he pass on one of them? They were a perfect three. The only thing that would have been better was if James Hunter had been with them. I wanted the whole quartet. #HunterCaldwellSandwich.

"Alright," said Jack. "Looks like you've narrowed it down to two. Do you have any questions for them? Or have you seen enough?"

Oh, please choose both Matt and Rob! I was devastated that Mason couldn't join us. But two out of three was still good. I bit my lip as I stared at them.

Rob winked at me.

"Hmm...let's see. Fuck you, fuck you, and fuck you." Chad pointed at each one as he said fuck you. And then he spun on his heel and stomped out.

"So…was that three passes?" asked Mason. "Or was he telling you to fuck all three of us? I think it was probably that one." He smiled at me.

I laughed. "He's just being testy. But I can be quite persuasive, so I'm pretty sure I'll be back soon." I blew them a kiss and ran after Chad. "Babe?" I called. "Where'd you go?"

Jack pointed in the opposite direction of the exit. "I think he got turned around and went towards the sauna."

The air got even thicker as I went deeper into the bathroom. I started opening sauna doors looking for Chad.

"I'm over here," said Chad just as I was about to open another sauna.

"Oh, hey babe. Why'd you come back here? Looking for more guys?"

"No. I just got turned around."

"So does that mean you're gonna change your mind and choose one of those guys?" *Please.* It was kind of a fantasy of mine to fuck a Hunter and a Caldwell. But I never imagined I'd get them both at the same time.

"Hell no," said Chad.

I tried my best not to pout. "Then who am I gonna blow? It's not like we're just gonna stumble upon the perfect option." Just as I finished my sentence, the sauna door swung open and someone barreled into me.

I almost fell over, but a strong arm reached out and caught me. I'd never seen anyone move so fast. In fact, the movement was so quick that it set me off balance the other way and I stumbled right into him.

Oh my God.

He was slick with sweat. But it wasn't bad sweat. It was sexy, good-smelling man sweat. I couldn't really focus on that though, because it felt like a toddler's arm was squished between me and his thighs.

Did I just kill a child?!

I stepped back and looked down. And I immediately re-alized what I'd been feeling. Because under his towel, I could see the outline of a huge cock. Were all the members of the Gryphon Club this well hung? It must have been a secret requirement.

"Play!" I yelled just as Chad yelled, "Pass!"

We looked at each other.

Oops. I'd been trying to always let Chad choose first so he wouldn't realize how badly I wanted to suck a huge cock.

And as I took a second and shifted my gaze upwards, I realized that this wasn't just any huge cock. This huge cock belonged to Flash Robinson. One head of the three headed monster!

"Did you just say play?" asked Chad.

"Yeah. I uh…didn't want to miss out on our final op-tion. I'm more concerned about why you said pass so quickly. I know you said you aren't a racist, but…"

Chad shook his head. "Babe, I'm not a racist."

"So…is it a play then?"

Please, please, please!

Flash looked deeply confused. "I feel like I walked into the middle of something very weird." He gave me the up down. "But you're hot as shit, so I guess I'll just stand here and see what happens."

"It is *definitely* a pass," said Chad. "Because I'm friends with his quarterback. Not because I'm racist."

"So you *are* racist?" asked Flash. "That's messed up."

"What? No. I said I'm *not* racist."

"Actually, babe," I said. "I'm gonna have to agree with him on this one. You did kind of admit to being racist."

"Yeah," agreed Flash. "You said you're both friends with my quarterback and a racist. But the former was your reason for passing on me. Speaking of which…what the hell does that even mean?"

"I'm not racist," repeated Chad. "I have a black friend."

Oh no. "Do you know how you could really prove how unracist you are?" I looked down at Flash's bulge.

"By donating to the NAACP?" asked Chad.

Flash nodded. "That would be a lovely gesture."

"Done," said Chad. "Now if you'll excuse us…" He grabbed my arm and pulled me out of the sauna.

"What'd I miss?" asked Jack when we got back to the lockers.

"Oh, not much," I said. "Just Chad being racist. Seriously, babe. First your reaction to me rushing an all-black sorority, and now this?"

Chad sighed. "That is not what happened."

"Then how do you explain yelling pass the second you saw him?"

"Did you really not see the size of his dick?"

"No…" I lied.

"It was freaking huge! I'm pretty sure I just saved your life. You probably would have choked to death on that thing."

I wish. God, I wanted to jam Flash's huge cock down my throat so badly. "Are you sure? Maybe he just had a water bottle strapped to his leg. It's so important to stay well hydrated in the sauna. He's probably tiny."

"No," said Jack. "I've seen Flash in the shower. It's enormous."

Gah! Traitor!

"See?" said Chad. "I saved your life. You're welcome."

"So who are you gonna choose?" asked Jack. "Only 40 minutes until midnight."

Flash was clearly out, but there were still lots of good options.

"Wow, only 40 minutes?" I said. "That's not much time. We should probably go back to Rob and Mason and Matt.

Since they're already naked I won't have to waste any time getting their pants off. And they were all super horny."

"Not a chance," said Chad. "They had huge dicks."

"Yeah they did." I tried to give him a high five, but he left me hanging.

"I meant they *were* huge dicks."

"Oh."

"So penis size is your primary criteria for selecting a guy?" asked Jack.

"It can't be," I said. "Otherwise he would have selected Mike."

"Huh?" asked Chad.

"Yeah. Didn't you see him in his underwear?"

"No."

"Well, there wasn't much to see if you get my drift." Pushing for Mike may have seemed dumb when he was so clearly small. But I was never wrong about big dick energy. And Mike freaking had it. And also…Chad was apparently intimidated by big dicks. So it was Mike or no one. And there was no way I was gonna let Chad give up on his dreams. "I'm glad you passed on him though. He seemed like a real asshole."

"Fuck, fine. Let's go with Mike."

"Great!" said Jack. "Chastity, you good with that?"

I nodded and smiled at Chad. "Let's go get you into the Gryphon Club!"

Chapter 15

MY DICKS IN TWOS
Friday, Sept 20, 2013

Mike came to the door still dressed in his underwear. *God, those abs...* If he turned out to be a grower, then I was in for a real treat.

"Good news," I said. "I'm gonna suck your cock."

Mike's eyes got big. "For real?"

"Yup!"

"Wow, okay. Let me get my robes on."

"Actually," said Jack, "why don't you just throw on some jeans and a T-shirt? We don't really need to do the whole sex cult thing for this. It's more just about having a video of Chad sitting on the sidelines while you get blown by his girl."

"Got it," said Mike. He disappeared into his room and came back out a second later looking so fucking hot in his jeans and T-shirt. I couldn't wait to rip those clothes off him.

We all followed Jack back down to the sex dungeon in the basement.

"You were right," whispered Chad. "He really is small."

"Told ya," I whispered back. And then I glanced over at Mike's crotch. I couldn't be sure in the dim lighting, but it looked like the bulge in his jeans was already a little bigger. *That's right, boy. Keep growing!*

Chad's grip on my hand tightened as we walked into the sex dungeon. Seeing the round bed and hundreds of candles must have made this all more real in his mind.

It certainly made it more real for me. I was about to blow Mike in the freaking Gryphon Club sex dungeon. And it was gonna be on film. AND Chad was gonna be watching.

I was already dripping wet just thinking about it. This was like every girl's dream!

Speaking of every girl…where were Ash and Slavanka? Were they still in the control room watching? Knowing those kinky bitches, they'd probably snuck off to the locker room with a few of the hot guys from the control room. Especially if Ash had gotten her hands on some banana juice.

"So how should we do this?" I asked. "Should I blow Mike on the bed? Or should Chad lounge on the bed and watch me worship Mike's cock on that throne?"

Chad's grip tightened even more.

"Bed?" asked Jack. "Oh, you mean the sex altar? Yeah, it should definitely happen there." He walked over and sat on his throne. Then he stood up. "I've never done this before, but do you want to take the throne, Chad? This is your party, so it feels like you should have the seat of honor."

Chad didn't move.

"Go ahead, babe." I gave him a kiss and then pried my hand out of his death grip. "I promise it'll be quick."

"It better be." He reluctantly walked over and plopped into the throne.

"Excellent," said Jack. "Just a few reminders before we begin. In order for this to count, Chastity just needs to blow Big Mike until he cums. And we need to finish before midnight, which means we have…" He looked over at the giant clock on the wall. "Roughly 35 minutes. Any questions?"

I shook my head.

Chad shook his head too. And then he frowned. "Wait, did you just call him *Big* Mike?"

"Yeah," said Jack. "Big Mike. That's his nickname."

Oh is it now? I very much liked where this was headed. Big Mike walked over and slid his hand around my waist. His touch gave me goosebumps all over.

"Since when is that his nickname?" demanded Chad. "You didn't call him that earlier."

"Did I not?" asked Jack. "I'm pretty sure I did."

"You definitely did not. And why is he touching her?"

"Just relax, babe," I said. "I'm sure they just call him Big Mike because he's tall."

"He's not that tall."

He wasn't. Which meant that his nickname probably came from something else. I shifted a little so that my hip pressed into his crotch. And based on what I felt, I was pretty sure I knew where his nickname came from. *Yes!*

Big Mike yanked on my skirt and all the buttons unsnapped. The fabric slid to my ankles, leaving me completely exposed.

"What the fuck!" yelled Chad.

"Wow," said Jack.

Mike took a step back and admired my naked pussy.

"This is just supposed to be a blowjob," said Chad. "Why is he getting her naked?"

Mike put his hands up. "I didn't mean to. I figured she'd be wearing a thong."

"Nope," I said. "I'm going commando all semester in honor of General Orville Thunderstick III. And anyway, I'm about to see him naked. So it only seems fair that he gets to see me." I unclasped my bra and tossed it to Chad.

Big Mike's hands went right to my tits.

"Whoa!" yelled Chad as he jumped out of the throne. "Hands off!"

Jack got in his way.

I looked back over at Chad. "Babe, relax. He's doing you such a big favor. The least you can do is let him play with my tits a little."

Chad sat back in the throne. "Can we just get this shit over with?"

"Sure," said Jack. "Chastity, whenever you're ready…"

Oh, I'm ready.

I grabbed Big Mike's shirt and pulled it over his head. And then I dropped to my knees and reached for his zipper.

"Oh, before you start," said Jack. "I should probably mention one last thing."

We all looked at him.

"The Grand Gryphon *did* agree to let a blowjob count as sex. But only if it might lead to the real thing."

"What are you saying?" asked Chad.

"That she has three minutes to make him cum. Or…"

"Or what?"

"Or he gets to fuck her."

Chad jumped off the throne and grabbed Jack's robe. "You fucking asshole."

"Babe, it's fine," I said. "There's no way he'll last that long, so it's a moot point."

"Are you sure?" asked Chad, relaxing a little.

I nodded. "Think about it. When have you ever lasted more than three minutes?"

Chad released Jack and went back to his throne. "Fine."

"Honestly, I don't even need three minutes. I can do it in two."

"Alright, two minutes on the clock," said Jack as he punched a few numbers into his phone.

"Wait, what?" asked Chad. "I thought you said three minutes?"

"Yeah, but then she said she could do it in two." Jack motioned to me. "Better pay attention. I think she's about to do the big reveal."

I unzipped Big Mike's pants and then grabbed his waistband. This was it. *Please be huge, please be huge.*

"Ready to see what he's packing?" asked Jack.

I nodded. And then I pulled his pants down.

YES!

He was huge! I mean…not nearly as big as Flash, Adonis, or any of the Hunter and Caldwell brothers. But still like twice as big as Chad.

"Jesus," yelled Chad. He covered his eyes and fell backwards in the throne.

Jack and I both laughed. And Big Mike just smiled down at me.

"Everything okay?" asked Jack.

"Mhm," I said as I wrapped my hand around Mike's thick shaft.

"I was more worried about Chad," said Jack.

Chad was being so weird. Not only was I making all of his dreams come true by getting him into the Gryphon Club, but he was also gonna get to watch me give a super hot blowjob.

"What's wrong, babe?" I asked. I really didn't get it. This was a win-win situation for him.

"I thought you guys said he was small!" He uncovered his eyes. "What even is that thing? It's freaking huge."

"I'm a grower," said Big Mike.

"Yeah you are," I said as I stroked his shaft. I flicked my tongue out to lick some precum off his tip. And then I started sucking.

God, I loved the feeling of his warm cock in my mouth. His veins sliding across my tongue. His tip pressing into the back of my throat.

"Fuck," groaned Big Mike.

Oh, honey, I'm just getting started.

I picked up the pace and let him pound against the back of my throat a few times. And then I spread my legs to get lower. The change in angle let his entire cock slide all the way into my throat.

"Wow," said Jack. "Does she always suck cock like this?"

I always gave great head. But I was going all out for Big Mike.

I put both hands behind my back and bobbed up and down on his cock.

And Big Mike fucking loved it.

Chad, on the other hand, didn't seem as thrilled.

"Babe, what the fuck?" he said.

I pulled back and looked at him, saliva dripping from my lips. "What's wrong?"

"What's wrong?" he scoffed. "You never do that to me."

"I'm just trying to put on a good show for you."

"I'd rather you didn't."

"But what about the cameras?" I asked. I have to make sure I look good in case this tape gets leaked." *Fingers crossed it does!*

"There's no way I'd break my oath to the Gryphon Club. No one is ever gonna see this."

"So you want me to do a bad job?"

"Yes!"

Really? And then it hit me. *Oooooh.* It all made so much sense now. Chad wanted me to get fucked by Big Mike. He just didn't want to admit it. *That naughty boy!*

I was happy to oblige.

"Okay," I said. "I'll be a good girl." I winked at him and started sucking Big Mike again. I still did a good job for the cameras, but not enough to make him cum.

"Thirty seconds," said Jack.

Chad leaned forward to watch.

I pulled back and licked Big Mike from his balls all the way to the tip. And then I jammed him into my cheek a few times.

"Ten seconds…"

"Fuck, come on!" yelled Chad.

But I knew what he really wanted.

I picked up the pace, but not *too* much.

"Three, two, one. That's time," said Jack.

I pulled my lips off of Big Mike and wiped my mouth. "I'm so sorry, babe. I thought I could get him."

Chad leaned back and let out a huge sigh. "Can't she have another minute?"

"Sorry," said Jack. "But rules are rules."

I stood up and kept stroking Big Mike. "I can't believe you didn't cum. You're so bad!"

Big Mike shrugged. "I mean…there was a pretty good incentive not to." He grabbed my hips and tossed me onto the bed. The silky sheets felt so nice on my bare ass.

I spread my legs and looked up at him.

"Nope," said Chad. "No way. This isn't happening." He stood up and started to walk over to us.

"Babe," I said. "I just jammed that huge cock down my throat to get you into the Gryphon Club. It would be such a waste to stop now." And I'd been teased all night by all the huge cocks I'd seen. I desperately needed one of them inside of me.

"I don't care. Come on, let's go." He put out his hand for me.

He was really putting on a good show. But I knew what he really wanted. "I won't let you quit on your dreams."

"What do you mean?"

"I'm gonna fuck Big Mike. Whether you stay or not."

"You might as well stick around to make sure nothing inappropriate happens," said Jack.

"Nothing inappropriate?" asked Chad. "He's about to fuck her!"

Jack shrugged. "Fair point. But hey, if you stay, you'll be in charge. You can even pick the first position."

"I'm not gonna do that."

"I'll give you a little time to think," said Mike. And then he knelt in front of the bed and buried his face between my legs.

Oh God, yes. I had to grip the sheets to keep from moaning as his tongue swirled around me.

"What the fuck is he doing?" asked Chad.

"It looks like he's eating her pussy," said Jack. "Actually, *eating* may not be a strong enough word. It's more like feasting."

He wasn't wrong. Big Mike's tongue was so deep inside of me. And his lips kept brushing against my clit. Each movement brought me closer to the edge.

"I can see that," said Chad.

I locked eyes with Jack. Did he remember feasting on me just like this last weekend?

Based on the way Jack licked his lips, I'd say yes.

God, I'd give anything right now to moan around his cock while Mike kept feasting. I loved my dicks in twos.

"This does absolutely nothing to get him closer to cumming," Chad said. "So it shouldn't be happening."

"Then choose a position," said Jack.

"Damn it. Fine. Reverse cowgirl."

"Wow," said Jack. "That's quite the choice. May I ask why?"

"I don't want her looking at his face. And that position just sucks. I hope he has fun falling out of her every two seconds."

Oh poor Chad. It was just him that fell out because he was too small. I moaned when Big Mike thrust his tongue deeper.

"Uh…okay," said Jack. "Reverse cowgirl it is."

Big Mike didn't stop though. He kept licking and licking and licking.

I was so fucking close. But then Jack cleared his throat. "Big Mike," he said. "Let's move on, please. We're up against the clock."

Mike pulled back.

Damn it!

And then he lay on the bed, his huge cock pointing straight into the air.

And all of my sadness about him stopping immediately turned to excitement. I couldn't wait to feel every inch of him inside of me. Or to see the look of jealousy on Chad's face while it happened. Steam was gonna be coming out of his ears. I had a feeling he was gonna turn into an absolute sex god after this. Jealousy did that to him.

I gave Big Mike a few quick sucks to get him nice and lubed up, and then I spread my legs over him.

"Ready to watch her get fucked?" asked Jack. "I wonder if it's even gonna fit."

"Wait!" yelled Chad. "He needs a condom. I can go grab one from my wallet…"

"Babe," I said. "There's no time for that. And anyway, your condoms wouldn't fit on him." I grabbed Big Mike's cock and guided it into me. *Oh, God yes.* I was so relieved to finally end my sex altar virginity.

Chad's eyes got huge as he watched all eight inches of Big Mike disappear inside of me.

I sat there for a second. I fucking loved feeling so full. But I loved getting pounded even more. I slid up and then slammed back down on him.

"Fuck dude," said Big Mike to Chad. "Her pussy is a miracle."

"That pussy belongs to me," growled Chad.

"Not until I cum." Mike grabbed my waist and started guiding me up and down. Faster and faster.

Now *this* was what reverse cowgirl was supposed to be like. Not whatever bullshit I'd done with Chad on Daddy's fun jet last weekend. Mike was completely in control and I fucking loved it.

"Why are you moaning like that?" asked Chad.

"What?" I asked, but it came out as more of a moan. *Oops.*

"Like that! Stop that."

Mike sat up and twisted my torso just enough to get a nipple in his mouth. He started swirling his tongue around it.

"Oh God," I moaned as he gently bit down on my nipple.

"I think he's about to make her come," said Jack.

Yes please.

"He better fucking not."

"By the way, it doesn't look like he's fallen out at all," Jack said.

"His cock is too big to fall out," I said. "I don't think I could make it fall out even if I tried." I tried to get off of him, but at the last moment he grabbed me and slammed me down onto him. "Fuck yes!" I screamed.

"Okay. Nope. That's enough," said Chad.

"New position?" asked Jack.

"Yes."

"What's the call? Better choose quick or I'm pretty sure she's gonna come."

"Missionary."

"Damn," said Mike. "I was really loving this view of her ass."

I turned to look at him over my shoulder. "You like this, you bad boy?"

"Baby, I'm fucking loving this."

I arched my back and bounced up and down on him a few more times.

"Hey!" yelled Chad. "Don't call her baby! And I said missionary!"

Fine. I got off and rolled onto my back. Mike was on top of me in a second.

And this position felt just as good as the last. Especially when he grabbed my ankles and spread my legs as far as they would go. And when he leaned down and his lips met mine. I was starving for a kiss. Our kiss was frantic. I just needed more. So much more. I grabbed his neck to pull him closer.

"No!" yelled Chad. "No making out."

Big Mike trailed kisses down my chin and sucked hard on my neck.

Chad yelled at him again, but the hickey was already forming.

"He just fucking marked her," said Chad. "This is ridiculous. I'm leaving."

"Wait," I said, pushing Big Mike off of me. Chad started to get up, but I got to the throne in time to push him back into his seat. "Don't leave, babe. He's gonna cum soon. I know it."

"Is he?"

"Yes. He can't possibly last much longer… Oh God," I moaned as I felt Big Mike's cock slide into me from behind. I had to put my hands on Chad's shoulders to avoid falling onto his lap.

"Did he really just start fucking you when you're literally one foot away from me?"

"He's just trying to help us. Wanna play with my tits while he fucks me?"

"I just want this to be over. Seriously, how has he not cum yet?"

"I promise I'm trying," said Big Mike.

"Well try harder."

"Roger that." Mike grabbed a fistful of my hair to make me arch my back more. And then he slammed into me so hard.

"Oh God," I moaned. I was so close to coming. Why did Chad look so mad right now? I was putting on the best show for him. I moaned again. Mike was railing me so fucking hard.

Chad turned to Jack. "There must be something else you can do to make him cum faster. Maybe give him some Viagra?"

"Are you sure that's a good idea?" asked Jack. "That might make him grow even more."

I'd love that for me.

"Well then definitely not that. But there must be something that could speed this up."

"Maybe he could fuck her in the ass?" suggested Jack.

Oh! Yes please!

"No!" yelled Chad. "Anything but that."

Damn.

"Okay, no anal. I'll try to think of something else."

"I have to go to the bathroom," said Chad. "And when I get back, this shit better be over."

Mike grabbed my arms and pulled me up into an almost standing position to give Chad enough room to wriggle out of the throne. Chad stormed out, slamming the door shut behind him. But all I could focus on was Big Mike. The change in angle sent him even deeper. And then he sat on the throne with me on his lap.

"You like that?" he asked.

"No," I said. "I fucking love it." I pushed my ass against him as hard as I could. He was so deep inside of me. But I didn't get the sense that he was gonna cum any time soon. "How have you not cum yet?" I asked.

"I actually have a confession."

I stopped bouncing and looked back at him. "Yeah?"

"Yeah. So after you guys came to my room the first time, the thought of fucking you made me so horny that I might have uh…rubbed one out."

"Mike!" I yelled and swatted at his arm. "You're so bad!"

"I know, I know. I should have told you when you came back. But I also couldn't pass up this opportunity."

"Are you serious?" asked Jack.

"Yeah man. I mean…can you blame me? Look at how hot she is." He grabbed my tits and jiggled them for Jack.

"I can't blame you one bit. It's taken every ounce of my self-control to not try to join in." He turned to me. "The way your ass was bouncing up and down…I almost asked to take a turn."

I smiled. "I'd love that."

He groaned and looked at the ceiling, as if staring at me for another second would make him lose control.

"But I think Chad's head would have exploded. Speaking of explosions…" I turned back to look at Big Mike. "When do you think you'll be able to finish?"

"Yeah," agreed Jack. "I speak for all of the punch masters when I say that I *really* want Chad to become a member."

I bet you do. He was definitely gonna make good use of that invitation the second the initiation ceremony was over.

"I'm trying my best," said Mike, staring at my body. "Usually I have to wait at least like an hour in between cumshots. But you're so hot that I think I might be able to cum sooner."

"Aw, thanks! But we don't have time to screw around. We have to find a way to finish this…" And then I thought back to what Jack had just said. About wanting to take a turn. And I got a wonderful idea. "Wait here."

Chapter 16

CAROUSEL OF COCK
Friday, Sept 20, 2013

I walked into the control room, still wearing nothing but my gloves and my heels.

Every guy in the room immediately looked up from his keyboard.

"Hey boys," I said. "If you wanna fuck me, raise your hand."

They all raised their hands.

Damn right. "Now put your hand down unless your dick is bigger than Big Mike's."

A few of the hands went down.

Oh my God! Really?! That was impossible. There was no way all of these guys were so well endowed. "I'll know if you're lying the second I take your pants off. So let me say that again. Unless your dick is bigger than Big Mike's, put your hand down."

There were lots of grumbles as almost all of the hands went down. Only two remained.

I looked back and forth between them trying to choose which one. But really…who said I had to choose?

"You two, come with me."

Both of them sprung out of their chairs. They couldn't wait to fuck me.

"Stop," boomed a deep voice. The guy at the center of the control room stood up. "You don't leave those chairs until I say you can."

"But…" protested one of the guys.

"No buts. As your leader, I could never ask you to do something that I wasn't willing to do myself. So if she needs someone to fuck her, I'll do it."

"How noble of you," I said.

"Just doing my job."

"Mhm. Suuuure." I took his hand and led him back into the sex dungeon.

"Shit," said Mike when he saw us. "Am I being replaced?"

"Nope. Just wanted to have a backup plan." I turned to the hooded guy that I'd brought with me. "You weren't masturbating while watching back there, right?"

"I wanted to. But no."

"Good. Now are we gonna stand around talking all evening, or are you gonna fuck me?"

He pulled his hood back and I let out a little gasp.

"Master Hung!" He was one head of the three headed monster. And I was about to fuck him! *Yaaaasssss!*

"That's me," he said with a smile. The candlelight flickering made his golden skin look even more gold than usual.

He was undressing, but it was going too slowly.

"Hurry up," I said. "I need to find out if you're really hung."

"I just told you I am."

"I don't mean your name. I mean your cock." I grabbed the waistband of his pants and I was about to yank them down.

But then the door swung open.

It wasn't Chad though.

Instead, it was…

Holy shit!!!

"Adonis!" I yelled, running over to him. I jumped into his arms and he caught me, his strong hands effortlessly cradling my ass.

"Hey," he said. "I got your note."

"Then why are you wearing so many clothes?"

He laughed. "Sorry. I didn't think it would be appropriate to run around with my cock out."

"Uh…you're freaking Adonis. You should *always* run around with your cock out." I jumped off of him and started tugging at his zipper.

"I'm so excited for whatever this is, but first can you bring me up to speed on what's happening here? Specifically, why is Big Mike lounging on the sex altar with a raging boner? And why are Jack and Hung just sitting there watching him?"

"Chad came in his pants during the initiation ceremony. But I found a loophole that will allow him to still get initiated if he watches me fuck someone and take a cumshot before midnight. Chad chose for me to fuck Big Mike, but Big Mike is an idiot and jerked off right before we could get down to business. So I went and got Master Hung to join us from the control room. And then you walked in. So now I'm gonna fuck all three of you."

"Wow," said Adonis. "Just to be clear…when you say that Chad has to watch you fuck someone and take a cumshot…is he watching you take a cumshot? Or is *he* taking the cumshot?"

I laughed. "He better not try to steal my cumshot!" I flashed back to when he'd attempted to steal my piña cumlada.

Adonis looked around. "And where is Chad now?"

"He went to the bathroom." And then it hit me. *The bathroom! Rule #3!* Was it possible that Rule #3 was actually: Never leave your girl alone when you go to the bathroom?

I'd really have to talk to Slavanka about her translating. Mixing up one or two words was one thing, but this felt like a stretch.

It seemed like a good warning, though. I mean…Chad had gone to the bathroom and left me alone. And now I was about to get triple teamed by three huge cocks. Or maybe two? I glanced back at Master Hung. I still hadn't gotten to see what he was packing.

But that was about to change.

"Alright, boys," I said. "Let's get this party started."

Adonis and Master Hung were both about to remove their pants. But then I realized I was being so basic.

"Wait!" I yelled.

They stopped and looked at me.

"You can't just whip your cocks out all willy nilly. This has to be an epic reveal. We're being filmed!" I walked over to the throne and dropped to my knees. Then I beckoned them over.

They stood on either side of me and unzipped their pants. I grabbed a fistful of material in each hand and pulled.

Oh.

My.

God.

Two massive cocks swung out and hit me in the face.

Adonis was just as magnificent as I remembered. And Hung? Yeah. Master Hung was definitely hung. Just not in the way I expected.

He wasn't as long as Adonis. But he was so fucking thick. I was legitimately worried that I wouldn't be able to fit my mouth around it. Which would be absolutely devastating.

Can you even imagine? This was my big porn debut, and I might not be able to handle one of the cocks. I'd never be able to show my face in public again!

I grabbed both cocks and slapped them against my smiling face.

It was tempting to just start sucking Adonis. But then I remembered Rule #23: Never back down from a huge cock. #Fearless. So instead I opened wide for Hung.

Turns out I had nothing to worry about.

Because of course I didn't. I'm amazing.

I slid my lips down hung until he pressed into my throat. And then I pulled back and switched to Adonis.

I couldn't decide which I liked better. I mean…Adonis was perfection in man form. But there was something intriguing about the thickness of Master Hung. And his thighs were absolutely *jacked*. I bet they'd be able to generate a ton of power on each thrust.

I alternated between them for a minute or two. But really I just couldn't freaking wait to get to the main event.

I stood up and dragged them by their cocks over to the bed.

"Grab a boob," I said to Adonis. "Left or right."

He stared at me.

"To determine which of you gets to fuck me first. It's like a coin toss, only way more fun."

"What about me?" asked Big Mike.

"You'll get a turn. But for now, you're on the sidelines."

"Damn."

Adonis squeezed my right boob.

Yes! "Good choice. You get to fuck me first." I gave him a kiss and then got on all fours on the bed.

Adonis came up behind me and grabbed my ass. I arched my back and felt his huge cock rub against my pussy. Oh God, it was better than I'd even imagined. And I'd been fantasizing about it ever since I'd had it in my mouth last weekend.

Just as Adonis pushed into me, Hung grabbed my head and pulled me onto his thick cock, stifling my moan.

I was officially fucking two-thirds of the three headed monster.

Now all I needed was for Flash to come join. But alas…Chad had been too intimidated by his gigantic cock.

Oh well. There was no way this would only be a one-time thing. I'd get Flash next time.

Adonis thrust into me while I went to town sucking Hung. Each thrust felt better than the last. On the football field, he was known for always being able to read a defense. Apparently that skill extended to the bedroom. Because he could read my body perfectly.

By the third thrust, he'd discovered that I liked being fucked *hard.* And by the fifth he'd learned that I loved having my clit rubbed.

"You're so fucking tight," Adonis groaned as he pounded into me harder.

God yes. I was pretty sure I wasn't the only one that had been dreaming of this since last weekend. And all I wanted was more. Thinking about Flash made me realize that even though I loved my dicks in twos, I loved my dicks in threes even more.

I choked on Hung and reached out for Big Mike. He seemed so excited to finally be coming in off the sidelines.

"What the fuck?!" yelled Chad.

I would have looked over at him, but my head was currently being controlled by Hung's hands. And if his hands were strong enough to hold onto a football while being tackled by 300-pound defensive linemen, then my neck muscles certainly didn't stand a chance against his grip. Besides, I didn't want to move. I loved being dominated by him.

"Hey, man," said Adonis, still fucking me in perfect rhythm. "Good to see you again." He put his fist out for Chad to bump.

"Adonis?" Chad smiled and bumped fists with him. And then he frowned. "Wait, no. I take that back. We're no longer cool."

"What?" asked Adonis. "Why?"

"Uh…because you're fucking my girl."

"Oh, right. Just trying to help a future brother out."

"And who the hell is this?" asked Chad, gesturing to Hung.

Hung let go of my head and stuck his hand out for Chad. "Shaka Hung. Pleasure to meet you."

"No," said Chad. "I'm not fist bumping or shaking anyone's hand while they're inside my girl."

"Sure thing," said Hung. He pulled his cock out of my mouth and went for another handshake.

Chad stared right at his ridiculously thick cock. "What the fuck is that?!"

Hung looked confused. "That's my cock. Have you never seen one?"

"Not like that! Jesus. I leave for two seconds and this turns into a gangbang. Let me guess - Adonis has a baseball bat between his legs too?"

Adonis pulled out of me.

I moaned a protest and he responded by slapping his cock against my ass.

Chad stared at it, totally speechless.

Adonis waited a second and then grabbed my hips and thrust back into me.

God yes.

"Whoa!" yelled Chad. "Stop!"

"Babe," I said. "Why are you so upset?"

"Uh…gee, I don't know. Maybe because you're getting gangbanged by three randos."

"They're not randos. They're your future brothers. And I'm just doing what you told me to."

"I definitely did not tell you to do this."

"Sure you did. You said you wanted me to find a way to speed this up. And what better way to speed it up than to play with three cocks at once? I basically tripled the odds of someone cumming before midnight."

"It's a pretty solid plan," added Jack. "But you really should let her get back to work. The clock is ticking. And unfortunately Chastity can't talk and suck at the same time."

"He's right, babe," I said. "Why don't you just sit on your throne and enjoy the show? I feel like Adonis is gonna cum any second now."

"Good. Wait. No! Not good. I don't want him cumming inside of you."

"So you want them to switch?"

"Yes. Wait, no."

"Babe, you have to make up your mind! We're running out of time."

"Yeah," said Jack. "You're in charge, Chad. But you have to give better directions. Let's make this simple: which guy do you want to fuck her?"

"If Adonis is about to cum, then him. But he better pull out."

"And who should she blow?" asked Jack.

"No one."

"Are you sure? Time is running out."

"Yes," said Chad.

At first I didn't understand his reasoning. But then I remembered this thing I saw one time that looked super hot. Chad must have seen it too.

"Okay, boys," I said. "Form a line. And whenever Chad talks, I wanna feel a new cock in me."

"What?" asked Chad.

"Damn," muttered Adonis. He gave me one more thrust and then pulled out. And then I was fucking *full*. I didn't need to look back to know who had taken Adonis' place. It was definitely Hung. I'd never felt anything like this in my entire life.

My legs started shaking when he was only halfway in.

"Oh fuck," I moaned. Everything started to go black.

And then he pushed on some pressure point on my back just as he slammed into me. And my whole world shattered.

"FUCK!" I screamed.

"Did she just come?" asked Chad.

"Mhm," said Jack. "And I don't think the past tense is appropriate here."

He was right. Whatever Hung had just done to me had triggered the best orgasm of my life. It didn't even stop when he pulled out.

I rode out the rest of my orgasm with Big Mike's cock inside of me. If he hadn't been holding my hips, I definitely would have fallen over.

"This is ridiculous," said Chad.

"Sorry," said Hung. "My cock tends to do that to girls. Can't help it."

Meanwhile, Big Mike switched off with Adonis. He filled me with his huge cock.

"Yes," I moaned.

Adonis must have been taking notes on however Hung had made me come, because his motion was fucking perfect. My legs started to shake again as Adonis rubbed my back with his powerful hands. Everything everyone said about him was true. Adonis really was a god amongst boys. But not just on the field. I was pretty sure every member of the Gryphon Club was some kind of sex god.

"You better not come again," said Chad.

Which was a mistake. Because him speaking meant it was Hung's turn again.

Adonis already had me on the edge. So as soon as Hung thrust into me, my legs turned to jelly and I buried my face in the satin sheets, stifling my cry.

I wasn't paying attention to what Chad said, but he must have been talking a lot. Because I was pretty sure each of them had taken another turn on me by the time my orgasm ended.

"Babe," I said when I finally had control of my body again. "You're really giving me quite the carousel of cock here. And I'm not complaining. But you might wanna give them each a bit more time with me before making them switch."

Before Chad could respond, the door swung open.

And my jaw dropped when I saw who walked in.

Chapter 17

CUMSHOT ON THREE!
Friday, Sept 20, 2013

No freaking way!

I was officially the luckiest girl in the world.

Because standing in the door was Flash freaking Robinson.

The third head of the three headed monster!

He must have come right from the shower, because he was only wearing a towel. And his skin was glistening. I wanted to lick every single one of his tattoos.

But mainly I just wanted him to drop that towel.

"I heard there was a party going on down here." He looked at me and smiled. "Mind if I join?"

"Sure," I said. "Get in line."

"What?" yelled Chad. "No!"

Big Mike pulled out of me and Adonis took his place. *Yes!* I immediately came again. God, Adonis and Hung together were the perfect combo. But they were only two-thirds of the three headed monster. I couldn't even imagine the orgasm I was about to experience when all three of them were going to town on me.

Chad didn't even care that Adonis had made me come. He was more worried about how Mike had gone to stand behind Flash.

"Mike, why are you standing behind him?" asked Chad. "He's not part of this."

Adonis switched off with Hung and went to the back of the line. Which meant Flash was next in line. Which meant next time Chad spoke…

"Hold everything," said Chad. "Pause."

Hung pulled out and started to switch spots with Flash. I was a split second away from finally seeing Flash's cock. Although his towel wasn't doing much to hide the shape of it. And it was growing by the second.

"Time out!" yelled Chad at the top of his lungs.

Apparently that was a phrase they recognized, because Hung froze.

"Babe, what's wrong?" I asked.

"Him," said Chad. "He's what's wrong. He can't just get in line to take a turn on you. That's not how anything works."

"I'm pretty sure that's exactly how this game works." And then it hit me. "Please tell me this isn't a racist thing again."

"What? No. It has nothing to do with his race."

"Really? Because it kinda seems like it does…"

"But I've already let Hung fuck you," said Chad. "And he's half black, right?"

"I am," said Hung.

"Okay, fine," I said. "If it's not a racist thing, then what is it?"

"I just… I just think that four is too many. We only have a few minutes left for you to make one of them cum, so they each need to get proper attention."

"That's actually a fair point," said Jack. "Eight minutes until midnight."

"Is this what all that pass or play shit in the sauna was about?" asked Flash.

"Yeah," I said. "But Chad was intimidated by your huge cock, so he passed."

"This old thing?" asked Flash, dropping his towel.

"Holy shit," I said as Chad let out a high-pitched gasp.

I knew it was huge. But without the towel… Sweet lord. It was a work of art. The girth…the veins…the *length*. Absolute perfection.

I licked my lips.

"No way," said Chad. "I already said pass on him. And the rules were that I got to choose. So he can just put that towel back on and leave."

"But babe, we might need him. You do everything fast, right Flash?"

"Yup."

"Can you cum fast?"

"I prefer not to. But sure."

"How fast?"

"I would say like three minutes. But…" His eyes scanned every inch of my naked body. "With a body like that, you could get me in two."

I turned to Chad. "Did you hear that? Flash is gonna save us!"

Chad shook his head. "He most certainly will not."

"Tell you what," said Adonis. "This reminds me of a preseason game we had. We were down by one score with eight minutes to go. Flash had been sitting on the bench all day because Coach had caught him partying too hard the night before. We all begged Coach to put Flash in to help us seal the deal, but he told us no. But then…when the two-minute warning hit. Guess who he put in the game? And guess who scored the game-winning touchdown?"

"Flash?" I guessed.

"Yup. So let's take the same approach here. If none of us cum before the two-minute warning, we'll put Flash in."

"Deal," I said.

"Great." Adonis pulled Hung and Big Mike into a huddle. I couldn't hear what they were saying. But I didn't really care, because all I could think about was how badly I wanted to feel Flash inside of me. The final head of the three headed monster...

Flash walked over to Chad. "Don't worry, my man. I'm sure she'll make one of them cum."

"Sure, whatever. Can you put that thing away?"

"What should I cover it with?" asked Flash. "My hands don't exactly fit over it."

"Here," I said. I peeled off one of my gloves and tossed it to him. He tried to slide it onto his cock, but it just tore the fabric.

"Jesus," said Chad. "Is his cock really bigger than your arm?"

I shrugged. "Guess so!"

"Your towel is literally right there," said Chad and pointed to where Flash had discarded it.

"But I have to be ready when they call me to go in."

"They're not going to call you to go in. Put your towel on!"

Flash ignored him.

"Cumshot on three!" yelled Adonis. "One, two, three!"

All three guys in the huddle yelled, "Cumshot!"

And then they ran over to me. Adonis lay on the bed while the other two picked me up and lowered me onto his cock. Then they hopped up and stood on either side of me so I could blow them.

"Hey!" said Chad. "I said no more gangbang!"

"Are you sure you wanna risk them going one at a time?" I asked. "Because if none of them cum before the two-minute warning, then Flash is gonna jam his cock down my throat." I deepthroated Hung to get the point across.

"I'm not just gonna jam my cock down her throat," said Flash.

"What are you gonna do?" asked Chad.

I reluctantly pulled my mouth off of Hung. "Yeah, what are you going to do to me?" I winked at him.

"I'm gonna put you on all fours right in the middle of the sex altar. And then I'm gonna fuck you so hard that you can't see straight. And right after I make you come for the third time in two minutes, I'm gonna unleash the biggest fucking cumshot you've ever seen."

"Inside of her?" asked Chad, his voice cracked slightly.

"Damn straight."

"Nope," said Chad. "Wrong answer."

"You'd rather I shoot it into her eager little mouth?"

"I guess?"

"Well then you're in luck," said Flash with a laugh. "Because I'm gonna do both. But I should warn you. I'm gonna get it all over that pretty face of hers. And in her hair. And on her tits. She's gonna be fucking *drenched*."

Holy shit.

His dirty words combined with me bouncing up and down on Adonis' cock took me over the edge again.

My pussy clenched around Adonis as my whole body shook. I could feel him stiffen inside me. And Hung's balls felt tight... And so did Big Mike's.

They were all about to cum.

No! Not yet. Not until Flash has gotten a turn.

I got up and walked over to Flash.

"What are you doing?" asked Chad.

I ignored him and grabbed Flash's dick with both hands.

"What the fuck?" said Chad. "It's not time yet."

"I know," I said. "But he said he needs to fuck me for two minutes. And can you imagine me trying to fit him inside me without any lubrication?"

"But…" protested Chad.

But it was too late. I was already on my knees. I licked his entire length and then took the tip into my mouth.

Inch by inch I let him slide down my throat. He was so big that I even almost gagged a few times. *Almost.*

"Damn, dude," said Flash. "No girl has ever gotten this far down. She's a fucking pro."

Damn right I am.

"Two minutes," said Jack.

I pulled back and looked up at Flash. "You better give me that fucking cum." I stood up and dragged him over to the bed.

As promised, he pushed me onto all fours, right in the middle of the bed.

"You ready for this, Chad?" asked Flash. "Once I put my cock in her, it's not coming out until her pussy is filled with my cum. Are you sure that's worth joining the Gryphon Club?"

God, everything he said was so hot.

"Don't you dare cum inside of her," said Chad.

Flash ignored him and rubbed the tip of his cock against my soaking wet pussy.

"It's supposed to just be a cumshot, right?" asked Chad.

Jack shook his head. "The rules just specify that ejaculation is required. So as long as we have proof that he came in her, then we're good."

Oh fuck yes. I'd taken lots of cumshots. But no one had ever cum in me without a condom before. And I was here for it.

I arched my back for Flash. "Please fuck me."

He put one hand on my hip to steady me as he guided his massive cock into me.

"Wait!" said Chad. "I didn't say to do it!"

"Too late," said Flash. He pushed further into me. And when his balls hit my clit, I shattered.

Next thing I knew, Adonis was in my mouth. And Hung was in my hand.

I was officially getting gangbanged by the three headed monster. All three of them!

And Big Mike. He was in my other hand.

Flash and Adonis both pushed into me at once. It must have been like 22 inches of cock. Which was two inches short of my goal. I'd always thought it would be fun to make two feet of cock disappear. But 22 inches wasn't bad either. And it was definitely enough to make me orgasm again. My vision started to blur. I barely had control of my body, but somehow I kept sucking and stroking.

"Two orgasms down," said Flash. "One to go. And then the grand finale. Time?"

"Thirty seconds," said Jack.

"Alright, boys," said Adonis. "This is it. Hut, hut…hike!"

Mike and Hung gently squeezed my nipples as Adonis grabbed my head and jammed his cock down my throat. Flash finished it off by giving me the hardest thrust I'd ever felt in my entire life.

And that was it. My vision blurred. My mind went blank. All I could feel was pleasure. And cock. *So much cock.* All for me!

There was only one thing that would make me feel better.

And I fucking got it.

"Fuck," groaned Flash. His cock felt even bigger than a second ago. And then it started to pulse. Warmth shot up into me. So. Much. Warmth.

"Oh God yes," I moaned onto Adonis' cock. And he exploded too, filling my mouth with my favorite treat. Usually I would have pulled back so that he could paint my face with it, but I was too greedy. I wanted every drop.

And anyway, Big Mike and Hung had me covered. Both figuratively and literally. Because when Adonis finally pulled back, they both shot cum all over my face.

"Oh my God," whispered Chad. "You've got to be fucking kidding me."

I wiped the cum off my eyes and looked up at him. "What's wrong, babe? Did I not make it on time?"

"Annnnd…time!" yelled Jack.

"Ahhh!" I squealed. "We did it! You guys were amazing!" I high-fived Adonis, Hung, and Big Mike.

Then I turned around to high-five Flash, but he just kept fucking me. He was still so hard. I didn't know how he was doing it. But he had me moaning again in a few seconds. God, I wanted to ride him all night.

"Dude," said Chad. "Quit fucking her. Time's up. If you didn't cum yet, that's your problem."

"Oh, I came," said Flash. "I filled her tight little pussy, just like I promised." He pulled out of me and the warm liquid spilled out onto the bed.

"Fuck," said Chad. "You were supposed to cum on her!"

"If that's what you want, man." Flash grabbed his cock with one hand and pulled me to my knees with the other.

"Wait," yelled Chad. "What are you doing?!"

"Fuuuuck," groaned Flash. His cock pulsed. But nothing happened.

Huh?

It kept pulsing. And pulsing. But still nothing happened.

"Ready?" he asked.

"For what?" asked Chad.

Flash smiled. "This."

He let go of his cock, and it fucking *exploded* with cum. Somehow he'd turned all his shots into one mega shot. It went in my mouth. And all over my face. And in my hair. And on my tits. And then back in my mouth.

"Holy shit," I said when it was all done. I felt like I'd just taken a shower. *Of cum.* Warm, sticky, delicious cum. "How did you cum again so fast?"

He smiled down at me. "I'm a man of many talents."

"I'm gonna fucking kill you!" yelled Chad. He jumped off the throne and ran towards us.

Flash laughed and took off in the other direction. The other guys all followed, except Jack.

"How'd I do?" I asked as the door slammed shut behind them.

"Best initiation ceremony I've ever seen," said Jack.

"Aw, thanks."

He pulled the invitation out of his pocket. "You know, that blowjob that you gave me in the bathroom was pretty amazing. But I still wondered why the invitation had a suggested sales price of a million dollars per guest. Now I understand it."

I smiled at him and licked some cum off my finger. "Think you'll use that invitation later tonight?"

"I very much want to. But can you handle more cock tonight?"

I stared at him. "Boy, I can *always* handle more cock. The real question is if you and the other punch masters can handle me."

"You're amazing."

"I know."

"Want a towel?" He grabbed Flash's discarded towel off the floor and offered it to me.

"Hell no," I said. "I worked hard for this. There's no way I'm gonna just wipe it off. It needs to sit for at least 15 minutes if I'm gonna get all the benefits." My skin was gonna be *glowing* after this.

He laughed. And then he realized I was serious. "Um...okay. Well, I hate to ruin your routine, but if you don't go clean up now, then you might be late for the initiation ceremony."

"Gah, okay. Fine."

Chapter 18

ELITE COUSINS F
Friday, Sept 20, 2013

If I was a normal girl, it would have taken me like three hours to get all that cum out of my hair.

But I was me, so it only took twenty minutes. And another ten to do my hair and makeup.

And then I was back at the sex dungeon.

Chad and some hooded guy were standing at the entrance.

"What's up?" I asked.

Chad glared at me.

"What's that look for, babe?"

"Do you really have to ask?"

"Oh, come on. Don't be mad. I did that for you."

"Did you? Because it sure looked like you were enjoying it."

"I mean…of course it felt a little good. It was sex."

"With four guys."

"Tell me about it. That was hard work. And messy! But so worth it. Because now you're gonna be a member of the Gryphon Club!"

Chad's face softened a little. "Holy shit. I am, aren't I?"

"Yup! Just like you've always dreamed of. I'm so proud of you, babe." I gave him a kiss on the cheek.

The hooded guy cleared his throat. "You're on in three, two, one…" He gave us a little shove into the sex dungeon.

All the hooded guys were back in their original places. And there were a few new faces. *Ash and Slavanka!* My girls were back! I wondered if they'd had as much fun as me tonight. They were still fully clothed, and their hair wasn't messed up. So I assumed they hadn't. But at least they'd found drinks.

"Yeah, Chastity!" cheered Ash, splashing some of her drink into the air. "That's my best friend! I freaking love her!" I thought she was gonna totally freak out when all the hooded guys stopped chanting and turned to her. But instead she just played it off by shushing Slavanka.

I squinted to try to see what was in her glass.

Is that banana juice?! Those sly bastards must have heard how she got after a few glasses…

It was perfect, though. Because if Ash was drinking banana juice, then she'd definitely be down to fuck the punch masters with me during the after-party. And Slavanka was always DTF. *That kinky bitch.*

I smiled at my girls as the chanting resumed.

Chad and I continued towards the throne. Jack was sitting there waiting for us. He gestured for us to go to his right, and then he got up.

"Gentlemen," he yelled. "And ladies. Please welcome the Grand Gryphon!"

"I love the Grand Gryphon!" yelled Ash as everyone else launched into a super intense chant.

Yup, definitely banana juice.

The door swung open and some silver fox in a bomb ass maroon suit walked in. His feathered cape trailed behind him.

Jack bowed and moved out of the way when he reached the throne.

The Grand Gryphon swung his cape around and faced the audience.

"Brothers," he said. His booming voice carried effortlessly through the cavernous room. "Today is a historic day for the Gryphon Club. Please put your hands together for our new member..."

Everyone started cheering. Chad stepped forward and tried to play it cool. But I could tell this was one of the happiest moments of his life. And it was all thanks to me!

"Are you prepared to take the Gryphon's Oath?"

Chad nodded and I nodded along with him.

"Very good. Repeat after me. I, Chastity Morgan..."

"I Chastity Mor..." said Chad. "Wait, what? Did you just say Chastity Morgan?"

Yeah, what? It sure sounded like he had...

"I did," said the Grand Gryphon. "And it's nice of you to be here to support her, but please be quiet or I will have to ask you to leave."

Chad laughed. "You've gotta be joking."

The Grand Gryphon stared at him. "I would never joke about something of this magnitude."

"But the Gryphon Club doesn't even accept girls," said Chad. "She wasn't even a pledge!"

The Grand Gryphon cocked his head. "Oh? Correct me if I'm wrong, but I believe she entered the library by your side last Saturday. In honor of the great General Orville Thunderstick III, she has forgone wearing panties for the last week. She was on the winning team for the scavenger hunt, and at the victory dinner the punch masters deemed her worthy to continue. And unlike you, she was able to successfully complete the initiation ritual."

Holy shit. He's serious!

I totally understood why they wanted me instead of Chad. I mean...I was me. And Chad was Chad.

So yeah, the choice made sense.

But this was Chad's dream. I didn't need the Gryphon Club to be amazing and successful. Chad did. And if he wasn't a member, then he wouldn't be able to introduce me to Rob and Mason and Matt and James and all the other hot guys in the Gryphon Club.

Wait a second!

I was gonna be a member. Which meant I could just introduce myself to all the hot guys.

And it would only take a few blowjobs to make them agree to let Chad in too. He'd be a member in no time. And maybe next time he wouldn't jizz his pants during the initiation ceremony.

This was really a win-win for everyone involved.

Chad started to say something else, but I cut him off. "It's okay, babe," I whispered. "I'll make sure they let you in too. It'll just take some schmoozing."

"May I continue?" asked the Grand Gryphon.

"Trust me," I whispered. I squeezed Chad's hand and we both nodded to the Grand Gryphon.

"Good. Now…as I was saying… Chastity, please repeat after me. I, Chastity Morgan…"

"I Chastity Morgan…"

"…swear to always put the brothers of the Gryphon Club first. I shall treat them as if they are my flesh and blood. And I shall never betray them."

I repeated it. But now I was wondering if they became my own flesh and blood…did that make it bad to fuck all of them? *Nah.* Being part of the same final club would make us as related as stepsiblings at the most. Besides, as every good historian knows…even cousin fucking is okay sometimes when you're elite. #EliteCousinsF. Besides, ala Single Girl Rule #8: If a man has 8 abs and 8 inches, he may not be refused. And they all had those.

"Then by the power vested in me by the brothers of the Gryphon Club, I hereby pronounce you the newest, and only, *sister* of the Gryphon Club. Welcome!"

"Yeah!" yelled Ash. "I love my best friend!"

Epilogue

KIDNAPPED!?
Saturday - Oct 10, 2026

"There's no way I actually yelled that," said Ash.

"You definitely did," I said. "Do you really not remember? Oh, right. Banana juice."

Ash's eyes got big. "Oh no. No, no, no."

"What's wrong?"

"At the start of this story you said that something wild was gonna happen in the bathroom. Like…even wilder than the banana party."

"Right. I was getting to that."

"Just rip the Band-Aid off and tell it to me straight. I got drunk on banana juice and then we orgied the punch masters in the bathroom, right?"

"Orgied?" I asked. "Is that even a word?"

"I don't know! I'm freaking out!" She grabbed my shoulders.

"I'm getting to it. Just let me finish…"

"No! This story was already way longer than it should have been. I can't wait any longer to find out what happened in that bathroom."

"Gah, fine. You've killed the narrative momentum now anyway." I plopped down in front of the bookshelf where I first found the Single Girl Rules.

"So…orgy?"

"No. There was no orgy. Sure, Jack and the punch masters tried to use the invitation. But the Grand Gryphon had made *me* a member instead of Chad. So the invitation wasn't valid yet. Poor Jack looked so sad when he realized he wasn't gonna get to bang me."

"Seriously? Then what happened in the bathroom?" Ash sat down next to me.

"Oh. You got kidnapped."

"WHAT?!" She fell backwards and nearly knocked over the entire shelf of Russian lit.

"Yeah. I was busy flirting with members to see if I could get any hot goss about what was going on with Chad's family's finances. To see if Teddybear was telling the truth about Chad's diabolical plan to steal all Daddy's money. Anyway, you slipped away to go to the bathroom. And that was when the Banana King bagged you."

Ash just stared at me.

And then something hit me. "Holy shit! I just realized something crazy."

"What?"

"Rule #3. I know what it means! It's a warning that you should never let your friends go to the bathroom alone so that they don't get kidnapped. Who would have thought?"

"Chastity. You literally quoted me saying exactly that at least once during that insane story."

"Huh, I guess you did!" I went to give her a high five.

"No! No high fives. I'm freaking out. Because you told me that I wasn't a virgin when I got married. And then started telling me a story presumably about how I lost my virginity. Which ended with me getting freaking kidnapped by the Banana King! Did the Banana King take my virginity?!"

"Hmmm…" I tapped my finger against my lips. "I don't want to give any spoilers. But I can tell you that this next story - the story of Single Girl Rule #4 - does indeed feature you losing your virginity. And it's *epic*. Seriously. I think every girl dreams of losing their virginity the way you did."

"To a kidnapper with a huge dick? No girl dreams of that."

"Well, he definitely had a huge dick." I smiled to myself just thinking of Ash getting absolutely *railed* for the first time. "But you'll have to wait and see who the lucky guy was. Spoiler alert - you're going to freak the fuck out when I tell you."

Ash's eyes grew round. "Wait. Hold everything. Did Chad take my virginity? Or Scooter?!" She looked like she was about to have a heart attack.

"I said he had a huge dick, so I think we can safely rule those two out."

"Then who was it?!" She was practically screaming.

"Excuse me," hissed the librarian. "I'm going to have to ask you ladies to leave."

"That's not necessary," I said. "My friend here was just excited because I was about to tell her the story about how she lost her virginity."

"Apparently he had a huge cock," said Ash. And then she lowered her voice to a whisper. "And I *love* huge cocks."

I stared at her. *Did Ash seriously just say that?!*

The librarian looked even more shocked than me.

"You know what else I love?" asked Ash. "Your horned rim glasses. And Chastity's stories! But most of all, I love banana juice!!!"

Oooooooh.

Now everything made sense. That third glass of banana juice had kicked in. Which meant Ash was now in her "I love everything" phase of drunkenness.

Ash tried to take a big gulp from my empty flask of banana juice and frowned. "Chastity. This is an emergency! I need more banana juice."

"Shhhh!" hissed the librarian. "Do I need to call security?"

I waved her off. "That won't be necessary. We're leaving now."

"Yeah," said Ash. "We're gonna go to Grotto's. They have banana juice, right? And pizza! Ahhhh! I love their pizza!" She jumped to her feet and helped me up. "You can't come with us though. Because you suck." She blew a raspberry at the librarian as she ran out.

I started to run after her, but then I realized that I hadn't put the rules back. The translated rules and my membership card were just sitting in the original book. And Ash had left it on the ground!

I picked the book up and just stared at it. These rules had changed my life. And as badly as I wanted to keep living by them...I couldn't. I'd found the love of my life. The rules had helped me find him. And they'd taught me how to be a good friend. Someone else needed them now. I slowly pushed the book back into the shelf, knowing that whoever found them next...their life would be changed forever too.

Just kidding. Well, kind of. The bit about the next girl to find them having her life changed was 100% accurate.

But there was no way in hell I was gonna stop living by these rules.

I was a single girl for life!

Or at least for the next few hours. Because I hadn't walked down the aisle yet. And I still had a few surprises up my sleeve for Ash before I did...

I smiled, hiked up my wedding dress, and ran after Ash.

She didn't stop running until we burst into Grotto's.

"Banana juice!" she yelled at a guy in a red shirt who definitely wasn't a waiter. "And twelve cheese pizzas. Now!"

The guy gave her a funny look.

"Don't give me that sass, young sir. You'd want banana juice and a dozen pizzas too if you were about to hear the tale of how you lost your virginity to a guy with a huge cock."

He gasped and ran out the door

And with that, I began the story of Single Girl Rule #4: You can never have too many shoes.

What's Next?

Single Girl Rules Book 4 is coming soon!

But while you wait, you can get your very own Single Girl Rules membership card! And some to share with your friends.

SINGLE GIRL RULES
Official Member

1 Boys are replaceable.
Friends are forever.

2 Girls' night is every Friday.
No exceptions.

3 Never let a friend go into
a bathroom alone.

4 You can never have too
many shoes.

5 Have wine in your purse at
all times.

6 Always kiss and tell.

7 Pics or it didn't happen.

8 If a man has 8 abs and 8 inches,
he may not be refused.

9 If you hear about a well-hung
man, share the news.

10 All celebrations of important
life events must involve strippers.

For your printable membership cards, go to:
www.ivysmoak.com/sgr1-pb

The Society

#STALKERPROBLEMS

You know that Chastity is going to get her man (or men…), but what about poor, sweet Ash?

Well I have some good news… Ash has an entire series all about her wild journey to find love! And you better believe Chastity is gonna be there every step of the way to help her.

And yes, Ash is definitely going to still be abiding by the Single Girl Rules. In fact, in the Society, you'll learn about at least 10 more of the rules.

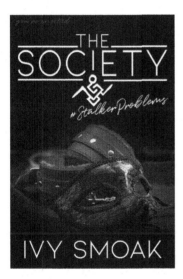

I got an invitation to an illicit club.

They say they'll grant me three wishes.

They say they'll make all my wildest dreams come true.

All I have to do is sign the contract.

Is it too good to be true? I'm about to find out.

Get your copy today!

A Note From Ivy

Was anyone else freaking out when Matt, Rob, and Mason showed up in this book? And kind of hoping that they were actually the #ThreeHeadedMonster? Girl, same. Because you know how I love crossovers. And getting to see them in college for the first time ever made me so happy. I probably won't be able to stop…

But more importantly, we need to talk about Chastity. I still can't decide whether I want a best friend like her or if I just want to be her. It's the last one. Definitely the last one. I used to always say that Ash was my spirit animal. But I've been really vibing Chastity's confidence. Just like I vibe a nice tan Rob butt. And my dicks in twos.

Based on that whole paragraph, I have definitely embraced my inner Chastity. I hope you have too. And I hope you're ready to keep reading about her wild adventures. Rule #4 is about shoes. But we all know Chastity can make a simple rule into something oh so very sexual. This next rule is actually what I've been looking forward to the most ever since I decided to start the Single Girl Rules. All I can say is that it is going to be epic. And will it finally answer a very pressing question…WHO does Ash lose her virginity to? Pop a squat and find out.

Ivy Smoak

Ivy Smoak
Wilmington, DE
www.ivysmoak.com

The Society

#STALKERPROBLEMS

You know that Chastity is going to get her man (or men…), but what about poor, sweet Ash?

Well I have some good news… Ash has an entire series all about her wild journey to find love! And you better believe Chastity is gonna be there every step of the way to help her.

And yes, Ash is definitely going to still be abiding by the Single Girl Rules. In fact, in the Society, you'll learn about at least 10 more of the rules.

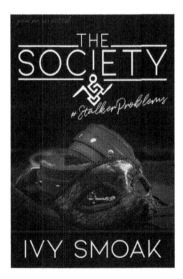

I got an invitation to an illicit club.

They say they'll grant me three wishes.

They say they'll make all my wildest dreams come true.

All I have to do is sign the contract.

Is it too good to be true? I'm about to find out.

Get your copy today!

A Note From Ivy

Was anyone else freaking out when Matt, Rob, and Mason showed up in this book? And kind of hoping that they were actually the #ThreeHeadedMonster? Girl, same. Because you know how I love crossovers. And getting to see them in college for the first time ever made me so happy. I probably won't be able to stop...

But more importantly, we need to talk about Chastity. I still can't decide whether I want a best friend like her or if I just want to be her. It's the last one. Definitely the last one. I used to always say that Ash was my spirit animal. But I've been really vibing Chastity's confidence. Just like I vibe a nice tan Rob butt. And my dicks in twos.

Based on that whole paragraph, I have definitely embraced my inner Chastity. I hope you have too. And I hope you're ready to keep reading about her wild adventures. Rule #4 is about shoes. But we all know Chastity can make a simple rule into something oh so very sexual. This next rule is actually what I've been looking forward to the most ever since I decided to start the Single Girl Rules. All I can say is that it is going to be epic. And will it finally answer a very pressing question...WHO does Ash lose her virginity to? Pop a squat and find out.

IvySmoak

Ivy Smoak
Wilmington, DE
www.ivysmoak.com

About the Author

Ivy Smoak is the Wall Street Journal, USA Today, and Amazon #1 bestselling author of *The Hunted Series*. Her books have sold over 3 million copies worldwide.

When she's not writing, you can find Ivy binge watching too many TV shows, taking long walks, playing outside, and generally refusing to act like an adult. She lives with her husband in Delaware.

Facebook: IvySmoakAuthor
Instagram: @IvySmoakAuthor
Goodreads: IvySmoak